Getting Rid of It

Lindsey Collen was born in South Africa, but has lived in Mauritius for many years. She was awarded the 1994 Commonwealth Writers' Prize for her novel *The Rape of Sita*, which was banned in Mauritius and resulted in death threats against her. This is her third novel.

Getting Rid of It

LINDSEY COLLEN

Granta Books
London

Granta Publications, 2/3 Hanover Yard, London N1 8BE

First published in Great Britain by Granta Books 1997
This edition published by Granta Books 1998

Quotations and adaptations from Charles Baissac, *Sirandann Sanpek:
Zistwar an kreol* (1888, reprinted by Ledikasyon pu Travayer, 1989) and
'Mor Lao Burik' from Charles Baissac, *Creole Grammar* (1880, reprinted by
Ledikasyon pu Travayer, 1990) appear with kind permission of the publishers.

'Light a Fire': Composed by Chris De Burgh
Original Publisher Crusty Music.
Used by kind permission of Rondor Music (London) Limited.
'Liberty': Composed by Chris De Burgh
Original Publisher Crusty Music.
Used by kind permission of Rondor Music (London) Limited.
'The Revolution': Composed by Chris De Burgh
Original Publisher Crusty Music.
Used by kind permission of Rondor Music (London) Limited.

A CIP catalogue record for this book is available
from the British Library

1 3 5 7 9 10 8 6 4 2

Typeset in Palatino by M Rules
Printed and bound in Great Britain
by Mackays of Chatham PLC.

To the brave women of Vallée Pitot

You just put one foot on this doormat and hey presto open sesame. No doorman. No questions asked. No magic words. Anybody could do it.

Even Jumila. Invisible waif and stray.

Note the distraction in her manner, see the panic rising to her throat. Like a snake. See her almost imperceptible limp. One foot light, the next one heavy, one foot light, the next one heavy.

She's not running away though. She's on urgent business, rather. You can tell by the way she moves quicksilver towards the door like that. One foot light, one foot heavy, one foot light. Like she's travelling just above the ground. Skimming it. She's harrowing her way somewhere. You can't tell if she's making progress. A ruthless pilgrimage. And her forehead's clammy. In one hand a bag. A white plastic bag. With *Air Islands Duty Free* written on it in red letters. The free hand wipes her hair back and pushes her shawl behind her shoulder.

She puts her beautiful foot, the heavy one, in its worn-thin sponge flip-flop out in front of her. A blue bottom sole, pink top sole, blue thong, just like everyone else's, stepping out from under her faded wedding trousers, on to this magic doormat. Shawl flying forward now. Forward, in the puff of smelly seawind that sneaked up the canal, got next to her, and tried to overtake her into the building. Face shining

1

copper with sweat now. Her beauty, because it's not just her foot that's beautiful but the whole of her, is unbeknown to her. Is her weight sufficient? Yes. Her weight shifts on to the mat. But then beauty doesn't matter right now because she's invisible. Any case, she's got enough, just enough weight, on the heavy foot anyway, to trigger the magic door. They call her a *seller of wares*. This is a thing she knows she is. She's got her card that says bearer-is-tuberculosis-free and everything, to prove that she's a seller of wares. She's left it, the card that is, with The Boy Who Won't Speak, who she's in charge of forever now, and who she's left sitting on the grass mat watching the bras on the upside-down crate outside by the Outer Islands Development Corporation godown. And there she is floating on to the doormat in front of the dark glass door.

It opens.

Slides to one side.

She's going in to see Goldilox Soo.

Goldilox Soo is older. Maybe around twenty-five. They say so. This is unbeknown to her. She's only got this name, no exact age. She's also beautiful. But she couldn't care less. Even if she wasn't invisible, she couldn't give a stuff.

Invisible, Goldilox Soo leaning her weight on her mop, as if to keep it on the floor, as if it might fly upwards with her on it and escape. She sees this other invisible being coming through the big automatic doors towards her. Shawl now flying in front of her. Sponge flip-flop stepping.

2

She waits like this just inside the big windowpanes, dark-glasses on the Millers' Group of Companies building, to see who it might be. Something about the light, then heavy, the light, then heavy, that rings a bell in her inner ear. Some recognizable pattern. The sunlight shining off the sea is so bright when the door opens, a slow-motion camera shutter and a flash, that at first she can't see who the invisible person is. One hand on mop, one on hip, she peers, her pupils readapting to the dark.

Oh!

She starts.

Then, Ah!

Friend, ah, Jumila, ah neighbour. Jumila. Pleasure. Of course, her limp. A limp more accentuated today. Funny, that.

Plans together for after work today. Today today today. Take destiny in our? False hopes. Today. Plans to attend. Plans to attend to. Plans assembling in her mind on her mop. They've had enough of it. Goldilox Soo and Jumila and Sadna Joyna, all three of them.

Goldilox Soo's jaw takes on a determined slant. Then, a picture in her mind's eye over her mop comes into focus of Jumila selling bras just outside the Outer Islands Development Corporation godown. On her upside-down crate. When the police don't shoo them away, that is, or man-handle them. Her and The Boy Who Won't Speak. But, wait!

Why's she here? The time. Not her time. The place. She never comes inside. What is this? She always waits outside,

3

waits till after work. Something wrong. The police again? Maybe. Or the Naked Midnight Man? No, she's not a believer in him. Or is it some trouble? Trouble in the kingdom. Right now, sooner than dreaded? Communal trouble, they call it. Murmurs. Bubbles. Gurgles. Burps. Volcanic groans? Hear the rumble? Tune an ear. Goldilox Soo has a *nose* for things. Things you can't even hear. Let alone see. But no. That's not here yet. Neither its sound, nor its scent, nor its fury. Today is still in time.

Goldilox Soo sighs, her weight settling on her mop. Her eyes straining to see Jumila.

Jumila floats in. She is seeing everything, the whole world, the whole universe, in faded black and white only. Then sudden dark. Inside. Strange, unknown, cold womb. Hand to clammy forehead tucking in the strands. Inside.

Then, when her eyes get used to the dark, in colour she sees Goldilox Soo. Halo around her navy-blue face.

'Ah, Gold. What are you doing here? You gave me a fright on your mop like that!'

Jumila steadies herself. Flash of warm relief dries her clammy forehead for an instant. Holds her outstretched hand, holds it right out, reaching, reaching, towards the figure leaning on the mop.

'I should jump. Not you. It's you who's come to see me, Jumila. What is it? About this afternoon? Today. Not today? No? Police? No? Then what's wrong, then? Where's The Boy Who Won't Speak?'

4

'I've come to see you.'

'What's in your plastic bag, Jumila?'

'Nothing, Gold. You free?'

'There's something red dripping out of the corner, what's in there? Of course I'm free.'

'Nothing much, Gold.'

'Looks like blood to me, Jumila. What you got in your plastic bag?'

'Trouble, Gold. There's trouble in it.'

Lucky they're invisible. There's trouble written on their bodies now. Double double toil and trouble. They might become visible and stick out like a sore thumb. And the blood

Drip

Drip

Drip

'You just follow me out of this place, with your mop in your hand, Goldilox Soo, and you just mop up after me, and I'll meet you on that bit of lawn out front by the canal.'

'Jesus.' It's Goldilox Soo whispering.

'And she isn't eighteen years old, when did she ever learn to talk to me like that? Or to anyone. What's she gone and done?

'And where's The Boy Who Won't Speak?'

'Maybe by the bras.'

Today. In big skyscrapers there are people who are going

about their business, as of right, and there are other people like Goldilox Soo who fall into the category of fairies and sweepers and *deevies* and cleaners and elves who are invisible to the others. If a fairy and sweeper and *deevie* and cleaner and elf gets a visitor, someone like Jumila, then she, the visitor, is also invisible. It bleeds over from one to another. The invisibility does.

Jumila turns around and glides back to the magic door
Drip
Drip
Drip
behind her
open sesame
and she is gone.

Goldilox Soo, still leaning on her mop frozen right there in that air-conditioning in the middle of all that Porlwi heat. Right in the middle of the marble ground-floor foyer dark-glassed-in from the outside. Stuck there with all these perspex partitions and a jungle of indoor plants and ferns and trees and a scary painting of lost in a forest by Stina Becherel behind her.

Five television sets on. In the air bookings behind her. Sound turned right down. Three tuned to 'The Mauritian Miracle'. CNN on the other two. Identical scenes change at the same time. Strange dance. Choreography. Silent films. In colour. Child watches heaps of corpses. A massacre in West Africa. With eyes that have seen too much. Seen too

6

much already. Perhaps seen too much last night. Or today? Today. A young newscaster neutral. Tired. Dead beat. An old man cries now somewhere in the ex-USSR, his heart wrenched out already, only sobs left in his breast. 'The Mauritian Miracle' three times. Changes to 'God saw Mauritius then He made Paradise', also three times. Just one channel away. Just the light press of a button, away from Rwanda, from Burundi, from Zaire. One channel away from the ex-USSR, ex-Yugoslavia. Ex-what? Today.

Goldilox Soo staring out at the canal, eyes fixed, scarf can't control her wild rush of, bush of thick hair, alarm bells of beaten brass, eyes riveted on Jumila. The stare of her black pupils out of the whites of her eyes out of her carved face is so intent, so stylized, so concentrated on Jumila, so focused on that girl's clammy forehead, so hypnotized by her plastic bag, that for a moment a passer-by stops. She looks right at Goldilox Soo, and the invisible becomes visible to her just momentarily, and she, the passer-by, thinks Goldilox Soo is part of the Stina Becherel painting.

She could be.

But in general she goes on being invisible to all those comers and goers of right. But some hear her murmur: 'Jesus.'

She glances around for a moment, abstractly.

'Be with you, Jumila.' Talking to herself now. 'Is today going to be postponed again?'

Goldilox Soo doesn't actually work for the Millers' Group

of Companies. She hasn't got a birth certificate for a start. They just get Klinnkwik in. Klinnkwik takes a building, or the public lavatories, or the courts, or the waterfront, or the Ministry of Finance, or whatever, for a fixed price, and they break it into square feet and take women to clean it for them piece-rate. Goldilox Soo is therefore what they call a Klinnkwik piece-rate girl.

But that is the least of her worries right now.

Now.

Now is pulling her out. Dragging her along. Insisting. Now is active. Now demands.

Right now is Jumila. Jumila standing out there with a plastic bag with Goldilox Soo not even knowing what's in it that's dripping blood into the please don't walk on this grass.

'Have to go see Sadna at her work.' The thought is there. In her mind already. Goldilox Soo sees that this a strange thought. Shudders. 'Go see Sadna.' She doesn't even know what's in the bag yet. But then again, she does.

So, invisible as ever, she follows in Jumila's footsteps, mopping the drip drip drip to the magic door, and then turns around again and prepares to go over, over somewhere, to park her mop someplace by the lift or something.

Today is the day before what they call the first isolated act of communal violence. The day before things, as they said in the press years later, were triggered off. Today is late.

*

At this point, the air inside the Millers' Group of Companies starts to firm up into jelly all around Goldilox Soo and her mop. An icy jelly. She has difficulty making her way through it. But she's got to. Got to go put her mop down.

'Is after work today already *too late*?' Goldilox Soo feels this thought like a physical premonition. Like it's somewhere outside of her, in that thickening air.

Their plans are out there too. They hang suspended now in the air before her. Balancing in that jellied air.

Goldilox Soo starts to move. *The now*, like gravity, attracts Jumila, and Jumila, like magnetism, attracts Goldilox Soo.

Today. The three of them intend to act. Intend. Today. This very afternoon. *Old oppression around too long now*, they felt it in their bones: time now for getting rid of it. *Start today*.

'Whatever were we thinking of?' she asks aloud. 'Who are we anyway? To think such thoughts.'

Now there's this plastic bag in Jumila's hand, with the red writing on it. And whatsoever may be inside it. A plastic bag powerful enough to put our plans in aspic.

The mop is heavy now too. No choice, she's got to leave it behind. Somewhere. She can't just roam around the streets with it.

Streets. There have been riots in the streets already. Riots you don't really know why. Sometimes a road accident sparks one off. As if people are inflammable. Tinder.

Inflammable. Public burnings of books. Already. Once because the prophet. They said. Then because the gods themselves were cross. They said. Insulted.

Insults. Too many. They play football at the Anjalay Stadium behind closed doors now – in case of.

And then right now there's blood dripping out of the corner of Jumila's plastic bag. Air Islands Duty Free bag. Will they notice my absence? Can my mop stand in for me. Hurry. Hurry up. We must act. Before it all separates out. Into colour and creed and bloodshed. Blood shed.

Could it be some crime?

Should it be buried? Poor girl. What am I thinking now? Panic stirs in Goldilox Soo. But everything's too slow for panic. Even panic can't go rampant now. Not in such air.

She feels her hair try to escape the scarf on her head. Spring out against that thick air. Oppose.

Goldilox Soo hauls herself, heavy, over to the service lift. Mop parking place there. She gets a fright, seen a scarecrow, seen herself reflected in some glass surface, mirrored on her mop. Fright reminds her of him. Of the Naked Midnight Man. A shiny and black and beautiful visitor who appears all of a sudden like that. He comes mainly to women, women and girls, and always at night and he can turn himself into a wolf, if that isn't what he already is. And then he disappears. Sometimes he leaves red marks on women's necks. Or he leaves young girls pregnant. So then men, men and boys, they make up bands and roam the streets with pangas, bloodthirsty.

It must be blood. Drip drip drip, out of the corner, the red colour of it.

And they say, people say, that there are people stealing people's children. To offer as a sacrifice? It isn't clear. Rumours are rife.

'Inauspicious times,' thinks Goldilox Soo. And, 'Maybe it's too late. Silly idea we had. Who are we anyway. What could we possibly do? Is now already late?'

Praying it isn't. She prefers calling on Mary. But anyone will do.

Invisible Goldilox finally parks her mop. It also goes invisible right then and there, between the service lift and the stairwell.

'**W**ell, what's wrong, Jumila? You said "trouble". Trouble in your plastic bag?'

The sun was so bright you felt nothing could be wrong. But a green fly came and sat on the grass under the Air Islands Duty Free bag, which meant there was something wrong. Something rotting. Directly under the bag, it sat. Wings blue silver black green. Just where the bag was dripping. Goldilox Soo held her breath waiting to hear.

'I didn't look at it properly. Covered in blood and blood clots it was. And I pulled the afterbirth out too. I'm still all shaky. Weak just under the knees. And my limp's got worse. And I don't know whether to cry.'

11

'You poor thing. All on your own?'

'I just put it all in a one-rupee plastic bag, a pale-blue one, I cleaned up the mess, and went out to bury it by the frangipani tree. You know, that stunted thing between my house and Sadna Joyna's. Between it and the dwarfed *peepur* tree. You know, where they said the Naked Midnight Man appeared just before he turned into a wolf.' As if the precise place would tell the whole story. As if a stunted tree or two could bear witness.

They lived, the three of them, on neighbouring shacks on government land. *Kowlenn*, it was called, from when it was called Crown Land. Now called State Land. They lived on the uninhabitable mountain slopes up behind Porlwi. Where floodwaters kept washing the earth away, making *dongas*, causing landslides in each cyclone, and now threatened to wash them away, bodily, and their shacks too. And even the electricity draped on rickety poles up the mountain, homemade, like a clothesline, too. And wash away their hire-purchase television sets. And their hairdryers. And rice-cookers. And themselves as well. If the police didn't get the squatters out first. With caterpillars.

The Government called them squatters. But the House Movement said they were State Land dwellers. Jumila and Goldilox Soo didn't know what they were for sure. Nor did Sadna Joyna. What they did know was that they were *illegal*. They each had an eviction order pasted with flour glue on their corrugated-iron wall by the front door to prove it. They had been warned. But then they had nowhere else to live. Who would live up in a valley on the mountain slopes if they could live on the flat? Who would like a goat climb up those slippery tracks? Who would choose to have an eviction order glued up by her front door? So they couldn't do anything about it anyway.

Their tin shacks didn't have more than six-inch foundations because of the rock. 'The mountain's shin', everyone called it. There weren't even storm drains up there. And the pit latrines so shallow that you couldn't throw a foetus into them for fear of being found out. The smell would give you away. You had to dig a new pit every six months, they said. Jumila, Goldilox Soo and Sadna Joyna had lived there for less than six months so they didn't know for sure yet. They would soon find out.

'Are you all right? What did you do? Why isn't it buried then? *Jesus.*'

'Nothing. I didn't do anything. I never did nothing. It came down by itself. All by itself. It was quite big already. I got a fright. I got a terrible fright, Gold. Feel my head, I feel weak. Feel how heavy it is.' Goldilox Soo measured the weight of the Air Islands Duty Free plastic bag on her right hand and felt Jumila's wet brow with the other.

'Jesus. You know you shouldn't wait till late like that. It's dangerous. You're all clammy. And you'll get sick. You'll get admitted to hospital. Do you want to die or something? And you'll get a court case, and a jail sentence. There's ten years in it. And shouted at by nurses and doctors and hospital servants. Please, please, Jumila, don't get sick.'

13

Goldilox Soo knew these things. She was, as you know, maybe twenty-five. And she didn't want Jumila to get sick and to die.

'Please, don't, Jumila. You went to see Madam Naga? Why didn't you ask me to come with you on the day? What if you keeled over on the way back or something? Are you sure she's got it all out?'

'No. I tell you, it came down by itself. All by itself.'

'You went to the chemist's and got Cytotec and took it?'

'I went to the chemist's but I didn't buy anything.'

'You bought those *latizann bazar* with the wild pineapple and god knows what poisons all tied in a bundle and stewed them up, put them to draw and strained the brew and drank it?'

'No, no, no.'

'You pawned god knows what and went to a doctor?'

'No. And don't you cross-question me either. I'm not a criminal, Gold. I'm just a woman. And I feel dizzy right now. Giddy woman.'

Jumila was what you call *learning to talk*. Talk as in talk back.

'Well, why are you acting like one then?' Meaning a criminal. 'Poor thing, look at you. There's a left-over question, you slipped and fell like everyone else in the slip-and-fall ward?'

'No. I'm telling you, no. I'd tell you the truth. I didn't *do* anything. It came down by itself. I promise.'

'You didn't tell me, though, Jumila. I didn't even *know*. A

14

pregnancy isn't something you keep secret, Jumila. And it's heavy already. And you expect me to believe you now, Jumila, afterwards?'

'Well, I knew I was pregnant, in a way. In my own body, I knew. I also knew we didn't use anything one day. You know how sometimes you feel carefree and thoughtless. And maybe the condom broke another time. I remember Rahim being worried and secretive. Anyway, I wanted it. I wanted this one. I wanted to keep it. I wanted to tell everyone. I wanted to tell Rahim. First, it's true, I did have two or three months of indigestion and nausea. My breasts swelled. Then, to confuse me, I bled a bit. I am so easily confused these days. Distracted. I put on weight. Then I didn't have periods. But you know how my periods have gone all mixed up since I left *him* and my little girl. And then I had another bit of bleeding. You must have noticed my tummy distended like that, come to think of it. Anyway, before saying anything I thought I'd go to the chemist's for a test, to be sure, you know, hundred per cent sure, because I was so pleased. But the test came out negative. So I thought I wasn't, in that case. I couldn't be. I've got the results with me. Folded up in my bra. I'll show you. So then this morning, at least a month after the test and my tummy getting quite taut, these terrible cramps started, and the bleeding. So it wasn't negative. So I sent The Boy Who Won't Speak to come in to town and get the bras set up, to get him out of the way. He wouldn't know what was going on. Then I crouched over this one-rupee plastic bag to try to

15

make less mess. My body didn't want to expel it. So I had to force and force. It seemed to take hours. I felt so alone. Sweating and moaning to myself. I thought should I go to the hospital, but there wasn't anyone to take me. So I just decided to get on with it.'

'Always just getting on with it,' murmured Goldilox Soo.

'Then when it seemed over, the afterbirth and everything, I stuffed everything into this plastic bag, stuffed a towel into my pants, went and washed my hands, and I went outside right then and there to bury the damn thing. Even before I'd cried. Oh, I wanted to keep this one. Since *he* took away my baby. Since I gave *him* his baby, I could say. I really wanted to keep this one. Rahim's. But it was all over. So I took the hoe, and looked for a spot between the frangipani tree and the *peepur* between my place and Sadna Joyna's, just where they say they saw him, and started digging. With a fury. I went mad. Digging and nearly fainting and digging.

'Then who should turn up but Koko. So he said need a hand, what you doing, so I said, oh nothing. You'll tire yourself out, he said. And I nearly keeled over. I was so pleased to see someone. I'm just equalizing the lay of the land a bit, I said. You know, equalizing. It seemed true enough. Flat again. And so he came and gave a hand. Nice man, Koko is. *Bon bug*. He didn't suspect anything. They don't, you know. He thought I was just equalizing the lay of the land with a vengeance. Some past vengeance. Some past vengeance that he didn't know about, or not yet anyway.

16

'Lucky I had hung the plastic bag on a hook by the tin door in case of red ants so he didn't see it. So after a while I said the land was equalized enough for now.

'Then when he'd gone to the shop for a drink, you know he drinks in the mornings now, I started digging again. And then this dog came and stood next to me, and I thought oh my god he'll dig it up again and pull it out in front of everyone. And then I got scared. I thought the police might find out. Or the courts. Or the hospitals. Or my brothers and uncles. Or even *him*. The world seemed full of people who shouldn't know. And me a criminal.

'So I put the one-rupee plastic bag into this Air Islands Duty Free bag and came down the mountain, caught the bus instead of walking, checked on The Boy Who Won't Speak and the bras and put my foot on the magic door and came in to see you. And you sent me out again because of the "What's in your plastic bag?" And that's the truth, Gold.'

'So now what?' Gold said.

She believed Jumila. Now she believed her. Relieved. To get rid of it was easy now that that worry was over. Or so she thought. At least Jumila wouldn't go and get sick on her, and start a haemorrhage or an infection or the gangrene and go and get even sicker and then go and die on her. It was just a practical question now. How to get rid of it. It was just a bit big to stuff into a rubbish bin in broad daylight.

'Isn't there any sort of place where you throw away things in this building, Goldilox Soo?'

'Let's see. The sanitary towel disposal thing has got this small ledge you have to put the Kotex on. Would be appropriate in a way. But then again it's much too small. For the other rubbish, they employ this Millers' Company man to check on Klinnkwik's rubbish every day. I don't know why. In case we steal through the rubbish system maybe. Or to sniff out industrial spies. Or whatnot. A bit dangerous. And there's the gardener's bin.'

Like Aladdin's genie, he turned up.

'Please don't stand on my grass. Can't you read, Goldilox Soo? You should know better than that.' The gardener, Dodonn was there, smiling.

'Your grass my arse.'

The gardener turned and walked off, smiling wider, pleased with the rhyme.

So Goldilox Soo and Jumila stepped off the grass, but Jumila kept the Air Islands Duty Free bag over the grass. And over the bag flew the green fly. Thank god for grass. Only one green fly. Blue and black and silver and green. Loud, it was. And threatening. Thank god for it being only one.

'We'd better go and see Sadna Joyna.'

She is the third heroine. She's just started work on a probation basis, as a hospital servant at the Civil Hospital.

She is also beautiful. All hospital workers are. Especially the hospital servants. Because they were there first. They know everything. Doctors come and go. Nurses get transferred from ward to ward, from hospital to dispensary.

Sadna Joyna knows everything Jumila and Goldilox Soo need to know.

And she's working days.

'Hurry because she's got time off for her court case today.' Jumila hurried on ahead. One light foot, one foot heavy, one light foot, one foot heavy.

'Be with you.' Goldilox Soo's navy-blue face shone in that sunlight as she looked at the sky. She noticed a wetness on Signal Mountain. Crying again, she thought. Silly mountain.

'Dodonn, hang on.' She ran after him. In her pocket Goldilox Soo had this circular letter that Giovanni had got at school the day before. She called the gardener back. His son was in the same class. At the government school.

'Did your boy get this circular?'

'No. No, he didn't. I don't think so. What's in it?'

'Look!' She had suspected as much. But she hadn't dared believe it. Not given to *all* the kids.

Goldilox Soo swore. 'I'm resigning.'

'What from?' Dodonn was lost.

'I'm writing to the *monseyner* and I'm giving back my baptism certificate. That's what I'm resigning from. Although I haven't got one. I'm resigning.'

'What you on about, Goldilox?'

'Listen to this, Dodonn: *Cher Parent, L'avenir de votre enfant est en jeu. Ses petits camarades qui font les langues orientales bénéficient d'une subvention de Rs180,000,000 du*

Gouvernement tous les ans. Les Catholiques n'ont pas un sou. Il n'y a pratiquement plus de professeurs Catholiques dans les écoles du Gouvernement. Il est très difficile aujourd'hui de trouver des volontaires pour le catéchisme. Il ne nous sera donc pas possible de faire la première communion cette année à votre enfant dans ces conditions'.

'I can't understand a word,' he said.

So she gave a Kreol summary. 'Dear parent, Future your child threatened. Every year government gives other little classmates doing oriental languages 180,000,000 rupees subsidy. Catholics don't get a cent. Next to no Catholic teachers left in government schools. Difficult to find volunteers these days for catechism. Therefore, impossible, under such conditions, to do first communion for your child this year.'

Dodonn just laughed: 'I don't understand in any language.'

Nor did Goldilox Soo. She started to run off after Jumila. But this time, Dodonn called after her: 'Gold! Hold it!' He came up close to her and said, 'Look at those posters when you go across the road after your friend, the seller of wares. Chill your blood, even in this stuffy heat.'

'Hands off our Vice Police Commissioner!' she read.

'Shiv devotees are right now demonstrating in favour of him. Right inside the Line Barracks,' he added. 'Posters not just here. All over the main island. Water Department subcontractors got their labourers to do it. My neighbour's one of them. It's a fact. There's a group, he says. Two ministers, three members of the National Assembly, the Vice Police Commissioner, some Cultural Advisors, heads of parastatals. Give contracts and tenders. Employ men.'

'Power and money,' said Goldilox Soo, not understanding what she was saying. 'And it might be too late. Today we've got *plans* you know, Dodonn. Plans to make plans.' Then she put her head back and laughed at herself. 'Fools, we are.'

'What plans?'

'Dodonn? Why stick to yourself? Why's your neighbour not doing something about it. I'm busy, Dodonn. Women's matters. And it's so late now. We're so late.'

'That's funny,' he murmured, when he saw four or five green flies on the lawn. Black and silver and blue and green. 'Bodes ill,' he mumbled. And looked at his watch.

'Yes, she's working days,' said the clerk at the administration section of the Civil Hospital.

'We know she's working days. Thank you anyway. We need to know the ward, please.'

'Eleven.'

Goldilox Soo recognized the ward. They call it the slip-and-fall ward. Ward Eleven.

They made it sound like a moral slip and then a moral

fall. It was a legal slip anyway. When a woman arrives there at the hospital in a bad state, she knows to say 'I slipped and fell'. Some even say 'I *only* slipped and fell'. So now the nurses and doctors say: 'Slip and fall?' Then the sick woman, agitated with pain and unnatural contractions, only has to say 'Yes'. Not add lies to her sins, Goldilox Soo thinks. Not add worries about what words to use for the cover-up. Not add any more stress to her already pain-ridden body.

And the doctor would say, 'It's OK. You'll be fine. Let's keep death at bay.'

Sadna was working on this exact slip-and-fall ward, they had just realized. Goldilox Soo and Jumila didn't know if this was an advantage or a disadvantage. But it did seem to be an omen of some kind.

Goldilox Soo, who had been right through primary school, and had written essays, said half-aloud to Jumila: '*Advantages and disadvantages of Ward Eleven*. Easier to dispose of, but there's probably more vigilance around.'

'What's that?' said the hospital clerk, not hearing properly.

'Nothing. Thank you.'

The Air Islands Duty Free bag was now inside another bag. This new outside bag had *Priba Paradise* written on it. It was a bag that Goldilox Soo had pulled out of her work overalls' pocket, like a surprise package. So now there wasn't blood dripping out of the corner any more. It was probably just dripping into the corner of the Priba Paradise bag. So they set off towards Ward Eleven. No one was allowed into the hospital outside of visiting hours, but in her work overalls, Goldilox Soo looked as though she belonged there. Or anywhere for that matter. She was practically invisible. And Jumila stuck to her.

Up on the balcony she was, when they saw her.

She came wheeling a trolley round a corner at high speed. Her body prancing out the message: 'It's today! Today is the day!'

Out of Ward Eleven into the wide open veranda leading from Theatre. Dancing. Sadna Joyna, laughing, left hand out to the side, as if in a ballet or some opera. Or an operetta. Blue uniform a tunic around her. Hair pinned up behind the blue thing on her head. She saw them down in the garden. Her hand was already positioned to wave wildly.

'Here I come,' she called loudly. The 'Quiet Please' rules don't apply to hospital domestic workers. 'What brings you two here?'

And, with that, she whizzed off into the lift with her trolley of laundry. Their neighbour. She and the twin babies. Also squatters on Kowlenn. She, also going with them, as if their lives were now plaited together, to their first ever *political* meeting. Today. This very evening after work. *Today*.

'Well I never did.' She arrived, stopped in her tracks. 'What brings you two here? Thunder, lightning or is it rain?' By now there were some full, heavy clouds building up, and rolling down the mountain, and building up again,

23

and beginning to roll down again, and a rumbling thunder in the far distance. And it was only morning.

'A foetus,' said Goldilox Soo.

'A what?'

'A foetus. In this plastic bag. In this Priba Paradise bag.'

'Yours?' Sadna asked her.

'No, mine.'

'She turned up at Millers' with this plastic bag dripping blood on the marble floors. Poor girl.'

'Oh, my god. Oh, my god.' Sadna put out a hand to Jumila's forehead to check for fever. 'Pain? Haemorrhage? Fever?' And while 'No, no, no,' she put her head slightly backwards, and flared her nostrils. Checking for infection. Clear. 'Oh, my god.'

'I'm all right. I'm still bleeding a little bit, that's all. I've stuck a whole towel there. I'm just a bit thirsty. And everything seems in black-and-white. Like old movies. Jerky too.'

'Well, call it *ours* now,' said Goldilox Soo. 'Hers and mine. We're dealing with it together now. And if you'll help, you can call it yours as well. What are we going to do with it?'

'Call a priest in to do a service,' said Sadna snidely, as if a squall had suddenly blown up in her. Her summer mood clouded over too. 'Yeah, call in a priest. Helpful in these matters. They register souls.' She was sarcastic, if nothing. Her dancing turned to a kind of stamping. 'They like doing the extra burial or two. They call it overtime. The Lord's own overtime.'

'Seriously, Sadna. This is no time for blasphemy.'

'Or go tell the gravediggers to dig a hole? Go to the Civil Status Office by the hospital gate, and get them to enter it in the ledger: found and lost: one foetus, sex, age in minus months from zero, and perhaps a ghost name. See if they give you a burial permit or a cremation permit or a what?' Fury built up in her. As if there was something about the hypocrisy that made her madder than a snake. Dancing snake.

'Don't be cross, Sadna. Be helpful.'

'I'll bloody well be cross if I want to. Making this poor child suffer like that over an abortion.' Anyone'd think Sadna was more than twenty years old herself. 'Could have killed her and you tell me not to be cross. Where did you get it done? Who by? Speak, girl. What method was used?'

'I didn't get anything done. It just came down this morning all by itself.'

'Go tell your brothers and uncles. Family! Yeah, go tell that religious brother of yours. And your ex-husband as well. They might dig a hole and hold a little homely burial service.' She got more furious.

'No need to lie to me. Keep your lies for the whole army of lie-collectors,' she went on.

'It's true, what she's saying, Sadna. I've had it out with her. It's true. It's that nice man of hers, Rahim's.' Goldilox Soo was trying to hurry things up now. Everything takes time.

Jumila lowers her eyes in assent. 'He doesn't know anything about it, though.'

Sadna quietened down. In respect. The squall had passed. A calm descended. They all stood there. As if at a graveside.

'Better leave it that way,' Sadna said. 'Let him be. They don't always understand. And they get scared.'

Sadna Joyna had realized it all. That Jumila had lost a wanted little one. 'My poor love. It's difficult when it gets up and leaves by itself like that. You feel lonely, don't you. And deserted. Are you sure you're not feeling sick. Ward Eleven's right here. We can go to Casualty and get the doctors to have a look at you?'

'No, I'm fine. And I've got things to do today. I'm busy. As you know. You are too.'

'You know something, Jumila, if you'd gone and had it done on purpose, there wouldn't have been this problem of disposal either. Come to think of it, I wonder what they do with the foetuses? All the backstreet abortionists.'

'What are we going to do with it?' Goldilox Soo persisted.

'And of course there's the police. They always interested in foetuses. They won't believe you like Goldilox Soo and I do. "Where did you find it?" "Whose is it?" "What sex is it?" "What age is it?" "Who did it?" "Where does she live?" "How much did she charge?" Blah blah blah.' She was beside herself again. The calm had been temporary. 'It's like policemen in bed with you and your man. Watching what will happen next. Waiting. Then pouncing.'

Policemen.

'And there's the reporters. *Découverte macabre*. Which reminds me, they had a little *"faits divers"* article in *Le Mauricien* yesterday afternoon. *Yesterday*. A patient on Ward Eleven's got it next to her bed right now. We were all sitting reading it together just before I took this trolley. An article about our ward, really. The bleeding ward. Look at all these sheets on the trolley. Women bleeding. Anyway it said: "Found in the Civil Hospital, a foetus in a plastic bag in a *poubelle* with the other usual detritus." So that's why I'm so cross, because I don't know what to suggest now. After this big hullabaloo. Nice thought you had: *hospital*. But here, they are all eyes for our sins, girls. We'll get arrested on the spot. Then we'll have to explain, and you know how that is. We'll have to get lawyers and everything. End up in the District Court.'

'Don't they have an incinerator, or something here?' It was Goldilox Soo. 'You know, for the appendices, the chopped-off gangrenous legs, the chopped-off hands, the cancers, the other foetuses, and what not? Do they burn them somewhere here?'

'Well, no, they don't. Not here anyway. Not anymore. Environment,' she said. 'Environment. Now there's this "offal" lorry we call it. It comes at night. I know the driver. But that's complicated. Specially after yesterday's article. I never asked what they do with it all. Perhaps they bury it somewhere. I don't know where, or burn it somewhere. I must remember to ask the driver. Samuel he's called.

'Let me take this trolley to the laundry van. Klinnkwik

27

does it now. Then I'm off-duty because it's my case today. Which is another reason I'm so cross. It's hard for me to take on another case. But then again, I have to. Yes, it's *ours* now. How big is it? You didn't tell me, Jumila. Mind you, you look pregnant. You never said you were though. God it's heavy.'

So, she went to take the trolley back. Signed out. And the three of them set off to look into the matter of canals and rivers.

It was only nine o'clock. So the green flies wouldn't start bothering them in a big way yet. Not in swarms anyway.

And there was a quickening breeze rushing down the mountain, and the smell of a change in weather.

'What's all this noise in the hospital? And a marquee? Sadna, am I going mad, is this a circus or something?' It was Goldilox Soo, staring.

'The hospital is. Prayer day. No one can say anything. Maybe that's why I'm being so quick to shout at you about calling in a priest. Close the hospital down and pray instead! I mean I've tried to object. Lots of the staff have tried.' Look at this petition, Sadna said, and dug a piece of paper out of her uniform pocket. They glanced at it: '*A chapel inside each hospital. Hospitals are not religious places. They must be secular space. The Church won't close it down, or hand it over to be used as a secular space. The chapel must stay, the Church says. Now a marquee for* kirtann *and* bajann. *Now an application to build temples and mosques. We protest. We*

28

protest against the presence of any organized religion on the hos-pital property. We, the staff and patients of the hospital, offer scientific treatment and care. In addition, we will not allow our-selves to be classified the whole time. Even when patients are sick. No shame. Religions have got no shame. The noise is unbear-able. The staff cannot work. Patients suffer. Call on the Minister of Health . . .'

'We haven't got time to read things,' Goldilox Soo said, tearing her eyes away from the bit of paper.

'I've signed it,' Sadna said, 'and I'm circulating it. I have got time.'

As they were going out, Jumila said, 'See this ward. When I was in the Surgical Ward two years ago, up there, they thought I had appendicitis but then decided I didn't, a group of some religious people came in, I knew some of them, and they said they wanted to adopt the ward. *Adopt the ward.* The specialist in charge said, "This, young men, is a government hospital. For everyone. Do you mind getting out." So they went away.'

'Not far enough away,' Sadna said. 'Look over there. See that plaque. They've adopted the Children's Ward over there. Look: the name of a religious organization on the wall outside the ward. Think they can do anything on the strength of they mean well. A children's ward. Children divided because these men mean well.'

'Could make you puke,' Jumila added with conviction, because she was feeling rather nauseous with exhaustion.

Also when she looked at the Children's Ward, she

29

remembered her little girl. With her ex-husband now, the one she calls *him*. Women, we're always producing, she thought. She looked at the bag now in Sadna's hand.

'Why don't we just throw it away any old where,' Sadna announced.

'Why not just here? It's not as if we haven't got important things to do today. The court case and the meeting. Stupid of us to ever even think we would be able to even *get* to this meeting.'

'And it's late. It's late. I can hear the sound of war getting nearer. Listen. Put your ears to the ground, girls. There it comes. Put your heads back and sniff the air, girls. Get the scent. It's got to be stopped by someone. And now we've got to get rid of this first,' Goldilox Soo said. 'Because it can't wait. A foetus in a plastic bag can't wait.'

'Being a woman,' Sadna said enigmatically, 'Being women. There's always this.'

Being a woman. Human being. Woman being. Jumila knew what Sadna meant.

Becoming a woman. Jumila stopped on the bridge. No light foot or heavy foot. Stillness. Dreamlike. Emptiness. Dizziness. Over a few seconds whole lives of hers were in her consciousness. Giddiness. What brought her to be standing here? Foetus in a plastic bag, feeling queasy, hiding from the police? From the public? From the doctors? From the magistrates? From the priests? From men? From *him*? Giddiness. Seeing in black and white again. Seeing an old home movie when she looked up the canal outside the hospital. Granular. Sepia. Reality hitting a mind warp.

With memories in colour.

'Whenever I see you, Rahim, my ears are filled with singing and light music. And deep inside my head there is a dance.'

'My whimsical,' he answered.

At first sight? No. Always. In sight and out of sight she carries him around with her. And he her too. Childhood sweethearts. They always knew one another so there never was a first sight.

But there were looks. Looks through eyelashes and long direct glances and then love-notes left in the contiguous wall and hands brushing.

She thought of him before she thought of herself. If you asked the question 'Who', Jumila would reply 'Rahim', before you specified what. And vice versa. In her dreams, it wasn't clear who the I was. Sometimes it was Jumila, sometimes it was Rahim.

Everyone knew they would get married. There were a dozen solid reasons. Like, same community same caste same religion same mosque same ancestral language same passport same race same ethnic origin same. Perhaps more to the point, same class. Their families were friends, not

31

like the Capulets and the Montagues. And neighbours. They lived in that bit of Plenn Vert that the Electoral Boundaries Commission has put into Constituency Number Four, for some reason. Anyway, to their marriage, there were no foreseeable obstacles.

'Some professional matchmaker will be out of a job,' people said. Their marriage was what everyone agreed it would be. A thing called a foregone conclusion.

He was two years older and not in any hurry.

He was wayward and would work when there was work and sit about on the edge of the pavement talking to passers-by in front of the tobacconists when there wasn't any work. From falling in love so young, so early, he had no highfalutin thoughts for himself. It didn't enter his head to compare himself with anyone. He went to primary school and then to high school. He stayed unambitious, and used to just read and read and read until his mother said this will be the death of you this reading.

And whenever he saw Jumila, he would tell her about all the things he read. So she knew more than people might think a seller of wares would know.

He stopped high school when he saw the cost to his mother. What with her sewing and sewing over her Singer sewing-machine and her eyes seeing dimmer and dimmer and customers not bringing their money as promised. And the Sundays sitting waiting for them to bring the money. And then they didn't bring it. He said he didn't like college any more anyway. And it was true in a way. All that competition that went on to beat the others. It was morbid, he said to Jumila.

So he stopped.

Instead, he thought a lot. About life and this and that. He listened in to old men talking and tuned out of the exclamations of the ignorant. He was an intellectual, a child of the enlightenment. How and why? They shook their heads at the difference between him and his big brother. Nobody can say for sure. A thousand little things, the women sigh. The mysteries of children growing up.

Big books don't know where they come from next to his bed. And dog-eared pamphlets by the television. And where do the tides come from and look at these ants carrying a cockroach up a sloping path. And war will soon break out there, he warned, and it did. He would put his cap on and be off, in person, to a strike meeting at the docks, that had nothing to do with him. Before the Socialist Party knew, he knew. It was said to be in his bones. He would be the one to tell them. Today at about twelve. Or, tomorrow round about three. But, when it was the fascist movement that got on the rampage, he would be cross and vigilant, pull his cap on right down, and go watch them from a distance. Hidden. Make sure I know what's happening, he said. He would inform his Socialist Party branch. He spied on the fundamentalists. Fundamentalists? Same thing. Only they're hypocrites as well, the lot of them, he said. And worse.

He fed a stray mother dog in the bare land that like an

old scar divided Plenn Vert from Sen Krwa. He stroked her head. But his big brother said they couldn't keep dogs anymore because dogs are unclean.

Women are too, he warned Rahim.

Rahim loved Jumila.

And they knew they would get married. Just like everyone knew it.

But she also had this big brother. And he decided one day and announced his decision: 'You're not going to marry that man. No sister of mine, no female of this family, will marry an atheist. Or a Communist. Infidel, no.'

He wouldn't hear of it, he said.

No one in my family will marry that kind of man.

Jumila couldn't believe it. Ever-fragmentary grouping, even Jumila could see that. Or was it just pretext. She didn't know.

She was silent. By silence, she meant no.

But he knew that you can make a girl's silence mean assent. She was only a minor in any case, so assent was not at issue. He knew that you can marry a minor off legally. Her mother and father were deferential to this brother. Scared of him. They seemed, she noticed, to bow down to him. He had beaten their father up. His father. The shame was hidden. The Code Napoleon gave prison for it. Not just a fine. But he had god. God was available for people like him to use.

Her family knew what Jumila felt.

Everyone knew her opinion on the matter.

34

Everyone knew her feelings for Rahim.

Only too well.

It was common knowledge.

But this particular big brother, who dominated the family, said marry her off the minute she turns sixteen, when the law allows, and he went right ahead and looked for and found a man from a village in the North for her and they did just that. She didn't even know his name. Had never seen him. And when she did see him, she felt a cold withdrawal in herself like from a toad. It wasn't his fault. But then it wasn't the toad's either.

He had a difficult time. For example, he had to all but tie her down on the marriage bed to impregnate her. This was expected of him. There would be sheet inspections and he didn't want anyone challenging his manliness in his house. So he impregnated her. Her belly swelled against her own will. And at quickening, she was torn between the movements which stirred an excitement in her flesh and her own willing the disgusting thing in her womb still.

When her sister's husband died, she, big-bellied, passed by right close to Rahim the day of the funeral. By the gate. Everyone was watching them, so he could only say three words. *It doesn't matter.* She smiled for the first time since the forced marriage. Right there in front of everyone. At a funeral. Big bellied and all. And then she half-accepted the growing creature, tried to accept it, *it doesn't matter*, used her conscious mind to calm her expelling womb, but she couldn't stop what went on deep inside, and deep inside the rejection grew.

Three months after having this one child – a measly, slimy little creature, that she had difficulty expelling, that was not expected to live, but that she learnt to love in a forlorn and gloomy manner – she tore herself from it and left. She left *him* and the still suckling baby. He *made* the child, she thought. And he was a good man. So he could have her.

She left *him* and her child.

They all thought she had gone mad, with the *post partum*, and they were too scared to do anything so they just let her be. Get her later, they said. You have to lie in wait for the young, they said. Catch them when they stumble into a difficulty.

But she hadn't gone mad. She'd just gone stubborn.

And so it was that she came to live with her widowed sister and her sister's nine-year-old boy, Tibye. This widowed sister, who had already fallen into a deep depression before her own husband's death stayed in it, god knows why, after his death. Maybe her insides, just like Jumila's, also stayed cross after her outside mind wanted to stop being cross. Anyway, her depression deepened.

So then one day, not one month after Jumila moved in, her sister just went and poured paraffin all over herself, doused herself like she was an old copy of the *Sunday Star* being used to start a rubbish-dump fire, and set herself alight right there and then in front of her son, Tibye.

He never spoke again. He probably could speak, everyone said. But he just *wouldn't* speak anymore.

Jumila's sister's rented house also burned down with her, so Jumila and her nine-year-old nephew went out into the world together.

Jumila and The Boy Who Won't Speak found work as live-in domestic servants at this historian and his wife's house. Jumila couldn't believe her luck. She had heard about the job from her mother's own sister, who lived on her own. Her aunt had wanted to take Jumila in, but the others threatened to have her house burned down if she did. No one was allowed to help Jumila. Unless she fulfilled a condition. The condition?

On condition that she return to her husband and her child.

So she didn't get help.

But now she had a job and a place to stay.

Her husband threatened to steal her back. He held out the baby girl, five months old then. She was tempted. But then again Rahim was in her ears and in her eyes and in her understanding. The baby opened its mouth and smiled, pulling her towards it. Then everywhere Rahim everyone Rahim pulling away. Then the baby.

It was The Boy Who Won't Speak who saved her. She had The Boy Who Won't Speak to look after instead. No. She said no. Hardened her heart. Against her own daughter. Her daughter would understand one day, she thought.

She decided to survive on her own with The Boy Who Won't Speak. Nobody wanted him anyway. This silent presence that he was. He reminded them of something they had done to his mother before him. Jumila found him a warm child, an understanding being, and a bond stronger than mother and child grew between them.

She and Rahim met there. In secret, at her mother's sister's house. This aunt wanted to help Jumila. So she left them on their own. She was like that. She was an adviser or a counsellor or something. No one paid her to do it. She just did it. A religious air about her. But the *maulanas* neither spoke for or against her. Two unrelated systems. She knew, it was said, the past, the present, and maybe the future.

She went off with The Boy Who Won't Speak for an outing, she said, maybe to the new docks to look at all the coloured containers, piled up like Lego, or to the old Garden to show him where slaves were hanged in public as a lesson long ago at the bottom of Plenn Vert and where no one sat on the benches till now. Blood marks the earth, she said. And off they went. The Boy Who Won't Speak's eyes gleaming with the excitement of the unknown. Of surprises. Of shocks.

So they were alone. Alone together.

Her mother's sister promised.

But then how was even she to interpret things when she didn't know *everything* there is to know, herself.

She said, 'You will be alone. Just the two of you.

A private time.' But then how was she to remind them of people watching. And of policemen. Policemen who keep watch on even the most private sex.

So they believed they were alone.

This is how it happened.

He closed the door and looked at her. She said can I undo my hair and brush it. Yes he said. And she stood up and did. Can I beat out a *sega* on an imaginary one-sided drum? Yes, she said. And he raised the imaginary drum to his left knee which was on the arm of a chair and did.

It started slowly and softly, the brushing and the silent drum-tapping, and then it became more and more abandoned and in time to the imaginary drum-beating, she brushed out her hair, and the brushing turned into a dance, one foot light, one foot heavy. The dance turned into the dance of love. And she danced and he played for her. She looked into his eyes with a look so direct and honest that he almost lost concentration until he summoned up the same look in his own eyes.

And then after reaching a calm climax, the number came to an end.

And they bowed to one another.

And laughed a deep laugh of love.

And expectancy of making love.

Love that was about to be expressed.

She put out her hand to him. And they marvelled at one another's hands. Let this take a century.

And in her hands she felt a deep warmth, almost aching,

in the palms and it echoed through her arms into her breasts and made her nipples stand on end against her bra. Let this last forever. A glowing warm fire.

And he spoke words of love, poems of adoration, to her and she listened. And the words caused blood to pound in her ears and to pass through her chest into her womb and down between her legs. As is the wonder of womankind. She was at her most desiring of him just fourteen days before her next period.

And as she passed her hands over his bare arms, he felt his heart ache with love, and his groin grow and tighten comfortably in his clothing in expectancy. Let this go on and on. His love, too, was linked to the moons, but he didn't know how. Perhaps she would teach him. Take him back to being a sea creature, now in the sea, now on the land, as the moon waxed and waned.

Love transformed their sexuality into eternal life. From the first sea change that stirred life into non-life and on into the end of time. Love linked them to the world of the past when life began and the world of the future where the unknown lies like an eternal gaping.

They were alone. Each of them.

At last.

Both of them.

Standing facing one another. Humans the strange standing mammals.

'You have been through so much. Married off, tied down, impregnated. You have given birth, and circumstance has snatched your daughter from your breast. Your sister has set herself alight and burnt herself down, and left you The Boy Who Won't Speak to look after. You are only seventeen.'

'And right now I stand and listen to you.' She, standing listening to him, the other. Humans the strange talking mammals. Listening animals.

'I don't know if I will be with you tomorrow or the next day or the next.' She went on. 'I know that up till now and right now I love you and I want to express my love. This can never be taken away. Let the future look after itself. Come and let me undo your shirt buttons.'

Which she did.

And he said, 'Yes, you undress me first.'

Standing humans being considerate of each other. Consciousness of me, myself, and you, yourself. Humans, being the strange caring mammals.

'No, just your shirt.' Then she took off her dress and her bra. And they touched one another's breasts. Where the babe feeds. There feed I. Where one generation joins another. The heart of the person. Hers full, his flat. And it was as though time stopped and a low divine hum, hum, humming-sound filled the universe. He kissed a birthmark on her ribcage. And she circled his nipples one by one with her tongue. And they stood out. Empathy of the male for the suckling of the female.

'Salt,' she said. 'Of the earth.'

Standing, she swivelled around and undid her *choos*

string. And calmly pulled her *choos* down and peeled her panties down and walked out of both and around Rahim. He looked at her as though she was a vision. She took his hand and placed it between her legs momentarily, and he felt hot warm wet, breathe in fast, and his own clothes tighten further.

Standing, she looked at him and put her hand to his belt.

'Yes,' he said. 'You undo it.'

She unzipped his fly as well, and caught his underpants in her fingers and pulled them down with his trousers.

He stood there. Vertical man, horizontal organ. Exposed. Tender. Vulnerable.

She vertical woman all roundness.

Two proud animals. Calm and beautiful and still.

He took her hand and passed the back of it over his collar bones. And squeezed her hand between his head and his shoulder.

She felt a trickle of her own warmth on the inside of her thigh. And then, as a sea breeze went through the room, the wetness cooled.

He knelt down, and then sat on his feet. Slowly he rolled a condom on. She smiled the smile of womanhood honoured.

'Yes,' she said.

He kissed the hair between her thighs. He palpated the swollen vulva lips. They tingled. His tongue touched her mons venus light as a dream and she closed her eyes and swayed.

She felt an aching pleasure pierce her ovaries one by one. A sucking motion began inside her depths. Her whole yoni felt at one with the tides and the moon and the universe. Time being born incessantly.

He felt a deep longing at the base of his penis. A longing which rose from between his bent thighs, and a twinge in each testicle squeezed upwards as he sat. The skin of his scrotum contracted and moved him. Up, up, his penis reached. Sea creature.

She stood her feet on each side of his feet, her knees hugged his flanks.

And then slowly, slowly as the sun sets, taking his hands in hers to steady herself, she bent her knees, they quivered unequally, she bent them further as she lowered her buttocks, opening her thighs, her yoni, her insides to him.

Slowly she aimed him into her.

First just the tip, and then she prolonged this moment of entry. Out of reverence for the sacred. In. And out. In and out. Like the tides. The tip catching on her contracting vagina mouth. Like the surface tension of a wave. Before it retreats. Over the reef.

And then she put her whole weight behind her and drew him into her completely.

They stayed still a while. Unison. Silence. Respect. Holiness.

Then moved up and down like a dolphin in perfect motion. She leant back. The burning heat of the pleasure rose. Rose and fell. Always higher. Wilder. Wetter. Hotter.

43

Slippery noises sucking. And just as a crescendo neared, she slowed and whispered:

'Let this go on forever.'

She held him still, moving just her muscles on the inside. Like the 'lup' of a heart beat. He too was still, moving just his penis on the inside. Independent of his body. Like the 'dup' of the replying heart beat. Lup-dup. Lup-dup. Lup-dup.

'Stand up a minute,' she said, moving him slowly out of her, and herself off him. She pulled him up.

She went over to the mirror, stood in front of him and they looked at their naked selves.

And were pleased.

'My eyes feed,' he said.

'It is as though we found something out that's hidden but is always there.'

He touched her clitoris. She felt a wildness.

'Please come in again. Now now now.'

Which he did, from behind, touching her all the while. And they both watched their souls meet in the mirror. A wild abandon took their bodies. Their mouths opened to the sky. Oh! Oh! Their hips berserk. Yes! Rising, rising, rising feelings. Total empathy. Joining of the universe with itself. The mirror shuddered with the orgasms, falling, falling, falling, dying, dying, dying, into outer space and utter peace.

Their knees shook, and they lay on the grass mat in front of the mirror, two child angels born.

'We have found innocence,' he said in her ear.

'Yes,' she smiled.

Someone must have seen him go. And then her mother's sister come back with The Boy Who Won't Speak. Or maybe they had seen him arrive and her mother's sister go out with The Boy Who Won't Speak. Or maybe they always suspected her. Who knows?

When Rahim went round to see her mother's sister, to take her her Friday's meat, he was that kind of man. Fetch an aunt her Friday's meat.

When he got there.

When he got to where the wall to her house was, he dropped the meat. He stood rock still. No! They wouldn't. They couldn't have.

'No!' he shouted.

'No!' he screamed.

Behind the stone wall, he saw it in disbelief, they had broken her house down and removed the rubble. She was gone. And Jumila? He panicked on two scores.

He picked up the meat and ran, ran in all directions at once. Asking the least offensive people. Where? What happened? Why?

'I don't know.' They all said the same thing. A chronicle learnt by heart over how many years of submission. A chronicle. *Chronique d'une mort annoncée.* But they said her aunt wasn't dead. Just gone. Gone for good. It had happened two days before. Two days after he'd met Jumila

45

there. Jumila was all right. Gone back to work.

But, she, they said, the aunt, she ought to have known better. Can't let these women do what they want.

Godmen. The Hisbullah. At night in four-wheel drives with cellular telephones chasing phantoms that travelled in four-wheel drives with cellular telephones. The devils and themselves fully modernized.

In the day, punishing women.

And of course, when somehow the condom failed, the sperm met the ovum, in secret harmony, as if defying barrier and reef, the police were watching. And the priests. And the magistrates. Just in case a woman put a foot wrong.

Like Jumila now. Standing in the middle of the bridge outside the Civil Hospital with her weight on her good foot.

They didn't need to exchange any words. There it was in front of them. Just outside the hospital, a thing still called a canal.

All along the southern wall of the hospital it ran, from the mountain side to the sea side. They walked down the middle of the bridge that crossed it from the hospital, drawn by some centrifugal force to the left handrail and

46

by some other equally strong centrifugal force to the right handrail. They stopped in the middle of the bridge. A hawker sold tapioca cakes in a glass box on his tricycle at the far end of the bridge. They all three moved slowly towards the railing on their right hand, downstream had there been water in it, towards the sea. Then they leaned over and looked down into it. *Just chuck it into the canal.*

Of course there wasn't any water in the canal. Just dirt. Instead of water, just swirling clouds above, rolling off Montayn Sinnyo, and getting pushed up again by a tuna-cannery-smelling northerly wind, a threat of rain, and far away thunder egging it on. Not enough to throw a foetus into. You can't throw a foetus into these signs that may become a gushing torrent by afternoon. Right now there was, at the very most, some slime here and there, oozing out of the bowels of the earth through the joins between the stones.

It was one of those old storm-water drains. A derelict ruin. Some memory of grandeur about it. Hewn basalt rock, massive walls. Same style as an old lime kiln built by the French East India Company. Now a sorry sight. Full of all sorts of junk. How many sorry sights had it seen? Accident cases rushed in and dead bodies being driven out from the morgue in taxis specially licensed to carry the dead. The offal van. But now staring at itself, it saw only household rubbish, plastic bags that looked just like Jumila's, dry leaves and green leaves, nondescript sludge,

47

dead hedgehogs, rotten mangoes, one particular plastic bag caught their attention because used sanitary towels were spewing out of it in mockery of their foetus, a washing-machine, old car tyres, all overlaid by more plastic bags, and potato-crisp packets and one old worn high-heeled shoe. Maybe there were already one or two foetuses in plastic bags down there. And a tomato plant stubbornly pushing through between two hewn rocks and grass and weeds and determined creepers getting a grip somewhere and persisting with green life.

They were tempted, all three of them, to just chuck it over the edge. One two three. There you go. Finished with the thing. Not make a production out of a simple miscarriage. They are happening all the time. Other women are managing.

But then, a canal with no water in it is a most uncleansing thing.

'I want to be cleansed of this thing,' Jumila murmured.

In any case, there were a lot of people just on the edge of the canal, people watching. People looking over the canal, as though it still had water in it. Leaning on the handrails, as if the two ponts that used to ply it long ago when there was water in it might pass one going up and one going down before their very eyes. The State Bank had a calendar with this picture on it. Where has all the water gone? And the best togs and the *ticas* and the umbrellas and the steps down to life on the canal? And the giant water lilies on the eddying edge?

The three of them stared down at the absence too. They were forced by their circumstance to stare at the new presences too. Because they had a decision to make.

It wasn't something you'd be proud to be seen doing, throwing a plastic bag with whatever in it into a dried-out canal. It would even look as if you were the ones that threw all that rubbish and garbage and junk in all along.

And there's a constant danger of accumulating fault, hoarding it up, invisible bit by bit, until you get guilty. You didn't want anything wrong to get into your actions at this point. Imagine being done for littering under the present circumstances. Everything could escalate till they got you for a hanging crime.

They were being watched. The people standing there watching them were all sorts. There was a young man who looked as though he had come from out-patients, practising in his head what the doctor had said and trying to make sense of it. There were two young women just stopped, watching the municipality workers cleaning the canal. Yes, there were municipality workers coming down, cleaning the canal. What if the municipality workers came over to the plastic bag when you threw it down, and then picked it up and looked inside, saw what it was, and raised the alarm? Cried, 'I saw the three of them. On that bridge.'

There's Line Barracks police headquarters right in view. What if there was a passer-by who had seen them throw it over and who could identify them afterwards. And then there'll be an investigation. Section 235 of the Criminal Code. It will be in the papers the next day: *Découverte macabre. Trois femmes interrogé par le CID. Foetus male dans un sac plastique. Complot délictneux. Arrestations imminentes.*

Not so easy.

All three of them leaned on the handrail. Let their minds wander off.

Jumila sweated and trembled. She wondered if The Boy Who Won't Speak was doing all right. He was just as good as she was at knowing a girl or woman's cup size. He knew all the prices. A regular client would hand him a bit of paper money and wait for the change. But he'd lose casual buyers. They're already timid coming up to strangers in the street right in front of the Outer Islands Development Corporation godown and talking about bras. They wouldn't stay long with that look on his face, those haunted eyes. And that silence. Customers like reassuring sounds. And looks.

Standing still calmed her. She felt better anyway now Goldilox was carrying the Priba Paradise plastic bag with the Air Islands Duty Free bag in it with the one-rupee blue plastic bag in it with the foetus in it. The clamminess got less. A bit faint. A bit dizzy. The same tendency for everything to go back into a faded black-and-white photograph for a few minutes, then old home movies, and then back to colour.

Goldilox Soo was wondering if anyone had found her invisible mop and noticed that her absence was rather

50

longer than usual. She shrugged. Only cut her pay. Life was so simple now she had her land and her shack. Didn't know why she hadn't done it before. It made her think of Sara. Sara. Sara. Sara. If Sara were still here, she could have done the same thing. So easy. Just up and off and stake it out. Could have made a house next to hers. Sara if only.

Sadna Joyna was preparing her court case in her head. The union lawyer had said she should think it all out in her head beforehand. Then the government lawyer would manage her case. What date she started work, and how, and who paid her, and how much, and the circumstances of the dismissal to prove it was unjustified and therefore that he had to pay. She owed it to Mrs Blignault. Get the bastard back. And to the Queen and Sheeba. No one ever brought to court for them.

But mainly all three of them had an unspoken excitement. Today was the day of the *future* for each of them. Their lives were going to try to be like a song that they would compose themselves. At least partly.

These chains to the present, the present, the present, and this being bound to the past, the past, the past, were going to be cast away. Today. They had decided to look forward, into the future. For the first time in their adult lives. Reclaim the future. As children dream the future.

It was Friday.

And they had plans for later. A meeting. Meet. Come together. Heads together. Think aloud. Meet others. Communion. Meditation. On mother earth. For tomorrow's

51

little ones. For ourselves. For every creature on the surface of the. And fowls in the air. And fishes in the oceans. Meet to work out. Meeting.

They didn't have time to think what would happen there. They had to *get* there. Even if they couldn't concentrate on a single thing that went on when they got there, they intended being there in person, in flesh and blood. Like the plastic bag was here with them right now, in flesh and blood.

'Are there other women in this socialist party? I don't like politics,' Jumila mused.

'How would I know?' Sadna answered.

'What do you *say* at a party meeting? Do you think it's *different* politics?'

'We'll see later, when we get there. Why do you think they invited us?'

'Will we ever know that? And what exactly is a party? They said it's ongoing. Not just for the elections?'

The questions and answers were circular, like a round robin.

But their decision to go was not.

It pointed forward.

'Look over there. What's that? What on earth's that?' Sadna Joyna was pointing across the length of the canal all the way to Line Barracks. There was a file of people going past, emanating self-righteousness and provocation, like a morbid beam. Young men and old women. All shouting slogans. 'Our Vice! Our Vice! Our Vice Commissioner. Shiv is with us. Shiv is with our Vice Commissioner!'

'Oh, Kali, where are you?' sang Sadna insolently.

Long ago terrible things happened in stories and nobody complained. They just knew that's what happened in that particular story. They thought about the meaning of it. These days, when you write a story, you have to be so careful. People can accept a magic door, invisible people, love at first sight, and that sort of thing, but there are other things they just can't stand anymore. They feel attacked. They don't know if you're just telling a story or somehow taking advantage of them. They get cross. Some of them do anyway.

These days, in a story, when parents go and die before the beginning of a story and leave two children, a son and a daughter, that is a brother and a sister, all alone in a house together, some people get cross with the writer on the spot.

They get agitated. A defensiveness gets into their voices. Their chests get tight. Their palms sweat. What if there's pornography in it? What if incest? They wish you hadn't chosen to write it like that.

As if you had the choice.

Another thing. Lots of people don't like things like axes in stories either anymore. Long ago any old story could have a bit that went 'And then he chopped off her hands at the wrist'. Nowadays they suspect this sentence. They accuse it. They say it smacks of wanton violence.

And people aren't used to foetuses being in stories anymore. They have been censored for so long now. Hidden in secretive gestures, not even amounting to whispers anymore.

They say things like foetuses haven't got a place in stories. You never know what might happen if they get into stories.

What some people don't seem to realize in all this is that there is the truth to take into account. And there are things that happen that have to be faced up to. Stories that have to be told. Like it or not.

Don't they realize it's more difficult for us, the storytellers, to tell it when it's like this? With risks of incest and dismembering and might-have-been-characters and I don't know what?

Can't they be a bit more understanding? What has happened to audiences lately?

And why don't they take it like a symbol? Can't they see that the brother and sister are parts of the same person now, just like they always used to be? Can't they see it anymore? Can't they just ask what hands mean in the story? What did they always mean? That foetuses are what could have been. How many could have beens do we lose every single day, without noticing it. Could have helped someone. Could have built something. Could have planned. Could have given. Could have opposed. Could have stood up. How many?

Audiences have gone suspicious of storytellers.

Can't blame you, in a way, if you're like that too.

Means I'm more careful now when I write. I put my ears to the ground in a story. I listen to the beating of my own heart in a book. I worry in case you're worried.

I've noticed. You touch your own breast softly. Feel if there is empathy in the story. You get in tune with the rhythm of it. You get in touch with the soul of the story. You trust, but on condition. And then you let go and you read and you feel.

Goldilox Soo and her twin brother's parents died, I don't know how, but the fact is there they were, a brother and a sister, twins at that, left all on their own in the house. No more than eight years old. Their parents dead and gone. Their father died first. Then their mother went and gave up and died as well. No use trying to get away from it.

Just listen.

Goldilox Soo stopped school and did the housework. Her twin brother took a job at the sugar mill at Lamek as a *chokra* but, after some years, the mill went and closed down. The Lamek sugar cane got taken to Medinn for milling. So, although he was only about twelve, he became a tree-feller. He would sharpen his own tools at home, his axe and his saws, and take on tree-chopping around the island. He saved up his money and bought a chainsaw. He was called

Tizan Tronsonez. He had his own ropes to make the trees fall where he wanted them to fall. On their Sité Valiji house was a sign which read: '*On desandre toute sorte de piès et couper de branches*'.

He and Goldilox Soo were identical. She always wore her scarf and he his cloth hat. Both were so dark you couldn't see them at night. But if ever he took his hat off or she took her scarf off, their hair emitted a golden light. As if they were luminous. They were good to one another, and got on well together. Whatever he had, he shared with her, and whatever she had, she shared with him.

One morning just before Tizan Tronsonez went out to work, he must have been about fourteen and Goldilox Soo, too, she said out of the blue, like a joke: I think you've reached the marrying age now. Yes, it's time for you to get married.

He said that he and she were fine together: No need, he said. Anyway I haven't got the time.

But she insisted. Don't come up with any nonsense about there's no nice girls left anymore. Look at me for a start! Go find yourself a wife. In any case, I need company here at home when you're out tree-felling.

He said he'd see. Then he added, isn't it time you got married yourself? You're the same age as me, he said.

She said no. Hadn't he just said they were fine together, him and her? And he went off to work.

But the conversation echoed a self-consciousness between them that had never been there before.

56

Goldilox Soo felt afraid. She'd been with him since before her birth. Cuddled against him in their mothers' womb. Fighting their way out together like that. Grown up together. Orphaned together. Living together.

Goldilox Soo looked up, scared, never had a period, and there was her brother's dog. Panting, pleased with himself. Covered in this thick layer of smooth green-grey slime from head to toe. He looked like a gargoyle.

'You've been at the swamp by the river mouth,' she accused him. 'Now look at you. Mud up to your ears.'

He wagged his tail, delighted.

'You'll be through the house any minute,' she continued in an accusing tone.

He was thrilled. Put his head back and smiled. Literally smiled.

She decided there was no other choice. She just went out up to him and grabbed him, her arms underneath his forelegs, hugged the slimy creature to her, picked him up into the air, his hindlegs tiptoeing on the ground, and carried him, slime and all, into the shower room and shut him and herself inside, and locked the door.

'Got you.'

She stripped her clothes off to wash them and to have a shower herself, at the same time. She would need it.

This was how she found herself naked with this muddied monster.

She felt she had just come out of a stinking swamp. Newborn. Reborn. With this muddied mammal as friend.

She baled water out of the bucket over him. He looked at her adoringly. His maleness came to her mind and stayed there, unthreatening.

But delicate was her balance. Poised, but only just. Precarious, after the conversation with Tizan.

Then she felt herself shudder. Not with fear. With the sensation of being an animal just coming out of the pre-historic sludge, with the giddiness of time disappearing forever into the past and then forever into the future. Endless. Infinity stretched. Made her head spin. Giddiness.

'Don't be overwhelmed,' she said to the dog, as if he were the giddy one.

Fear. Honour. Horror.

And then a strange, unrecognizable happiness.

So deep she didn't know where it came from.

Her nakedness was total.

A kind of peace and vulnerability settled on her.

And then, at that very moment, in that peace, she saw a green-brown snake slide out of the drain hole on to the shower floor next to her and the dog.

And it looked at them. Its body an S. A question. A query.

It too seemed to smile.

No forked tongue. No threat intended.

She looked down at it and said half aloud, down to it, addressing the snake in person:

'Thank goodness you and I are not swimming in the same swampy water.'

She knew that eye to eye in the water, she would have capitulated, given in to the fear and horror that she felt stir in her chest.

She waited for him to go back down his hole.

Of course, he did.

Then she washed the dog, washed her dress, bathed herself, and went on with the day.

The heat was beating down on their sité house in Valiji that day.

She loved their house. Not just liked, loved. She loved it. Where she and her twin brother had lived happily ever before.

It was a very hot afternoon when, without any prior warning, the pain started, then the cramps and the bleeding. She felt terror. She looked at her own body in horror. What is this, she asked.

She called out to Medze, her neighbour in the semi-detached sité house. Panicking. Ignorant. Medze realized at once, and said, 'Come to the shower room.' She got little Goldilox Soo there. And there, Goldilox Soo leant against the wall, put her head back, agitation expressed in her movements. Together they pulled out the clots and the tiny foetus and everything.

An early miscarriage it was, before she ever had a period. Medze held her hand and said, 'Don't cry,' and then, 'Yes, you'd better cry a bit. That's better now.'

Luckily Tizan wasn't there. 'Men don't like this type of

59

thing,' said Medze and the two women sighed. Goldilox Soo a woman now. So suddenly.

So she and Medze buried it in the back garden by the toilet. They put a big rock on it because of the gargoyle dog.

But Tizan got home from work, and he found out. The dog didn't actually dig it up. He just acted odd. So then Tizan went to see why, and he dug it up, and found it and started this ranting and raving.

'I'll chop your hands off,' he said. 'If you were my wife, I'd saw them off. I'll tell the police. Get out of here.'

He kicked Goldilox Soo out.

'Maybe it's all for the best,' Medze said, 'if that's what he's like. But where will you go, girl-woman?'

'And I half of a pair of twins,' said Goldilox Soo.

Some people said the pregnancy was Tizan's, that was why he was so cross. Others said he was just cross in case people thought it was. Others said that he was just cross because she wasn't married yet, and that he said he had told her she ought to be getting married. Other people said he had seen it was a boy foetus and he wanted 'his nephew', as they put it, to live and be a son to him. None closer than a sister's son, for men like him. He was only about fourteen himself.

So Goldilox Soo went out into the woodlands in the north and lived in a makeshift tent made from *vakwa* leaves. Like a runaway. A maroon. The gargoyle dog followed her.

Goldilox Soo's wrists were paralysed. Some people said it was the shock. Others naturally said it was evil spirits. The dog hunted down rabbits and *tang*, and she tried to pick berries with her paralysed hands. And they lived from paralysed hand to mouth for months.

One day she was down by the river trying to pick berries. She leant out over the river to reach some berries right at the end of a branch. She lost her balance, and would have fallen in, but her hands suddenly came back to life and she grabbed the branch and swung. The dog waited on the riverbank for her. An old lady was going past, saw her and the gargoyle dog and said: 'Where do you two live? In the woodlands? In the open air like this? Come and live in my house? You look as if you are with child, girl.'

Goldilox Soo and the dog went to live with this old lady in her grass hut. The old lady was quite right. Goldilox Soo never had a period, because she was pregnant again. Within months, in the woodlands in the north, living in the old lady's grass house, herself and the gargoyle dog, she gave birth to the calm Giovanni.

She sometimes made out that she had got him through eating too many wild green mangoes down by the river-banks, and sometimes she said that she, too, had had an immaculate conception. Most often, she said she knew as much about it as about the first pregnancy which had ended in miscarriage. The old lady told her that this type of thing happens in the woodlands. People born twins, like you were, are always looking for another twin. Maybe you met someone in the woodlands one day who you thought might be the perfect replacement for your lost twin brother and that's how you fell pregnant. Only you were wrong, he wasn't the perfect replacement.

'Take Giovanni,' she said, 'in the meantime, for what he is: a gift from nature. Look how clever he is, Goldilox Soo. Just like you. Look how strong he is. Just like you.'

The old lady took Goldilox Soo along to do occasional work for a small cane planter on a daily basis. They would do weeding, put down fertilizer, do *depayaz* and, in the milling season, cut cane. The other women labourers tolerated them, but did not befriend them. In case, through too much proximity, they also got looked on as witches by the villagers.

Goldilox Soo got her boychild vaccinated. In the name Giovanni Soo. And when Giovanni was five Goldilox sent him to school. Every year he did better and better at school. And every year he shone like a star in that northern woodland. He could hunt and fish and gather roots and berries. He could fetch wood and build a fire. He could carry water and plant fourteen kinds of edible leaves.

The old lady taught Goldilox Soo all she needed to know about life and death. Then after that, she died herself, quite quietly, after having said goodbye. The village priest, a soft-spoken kind man, agreed to do a funeral, although it wasn't clear the old lady was Catholic. Goldilox Soo pointed out that she was doing the funeral, and she was Catholic, only she didn't have a baptismal paper. And the women from work helped organize a coffin. They got men to carry it to the church behind a bunch of flowers held by Giovanni.

Soon afterwards the gargoyle dog went off and never came back.

It was then that Goldilox Soo opened a *L'Express* newspaper on the counter of the shop she bought rice from, and saw the advertisement put in by Sara's husband.

'I'm ready for that now,' said Goldilox Soo.

And it was then that she and Giovanni went to Porlwi. A maroon and her child, walking in to Porlwi with a change of clothes in her *vakwa* basket, and some money the old lady had left them, seeking a contract of employment.

The estuary. Let's go to the Grand River North West, to the estuary,' said Sadna, seeing a bus coming along heading in that direction. 'I've got enough time before court. There'll be gallons and gallons of water about, water by the cubic metre, running water, gushing, charging, hurtling, to whoosh it into the sea.' The dry canal had made them all thirst for water. Water water water. Cleansing water. For a burial at sea.

'That will be good and clean,' said Jumila.

'Enough of this talk of clean, clean, clean,' said Goldilox Soo. 'Wash away thy guilt? Why're we always guilty? On and on about *clean*. Are you tired, Jumila. Are you all right? Are you feeling weak?'

63

Jumila had images of fish studying the contents of the plastic bag. Cleaning, cleaning, cleaning. Healing healing healing.

She felt better.

'No, I'm OK. I'm just sad maybe. And my weak foot's weaker.'

The bus was painted like a chocolate bar with its brand-name all over the whole bus.

It started raining. A slow gentle rain.

Standing room only. Doesn't matter.

'That's good, the rain,' said Goldilox Soo. 'There won't be anyone on the bridge. Yes, I can see why you're sad. You wanted it. And your body didn't. Not yet anyway. Yes, it's worse when it goes by itself. Like you say, Sadna. Some people don't believe that.'

In the bus, they went on talking. But about other things. Talking and hanging from the ceiling. Goldilox was careful with the bag. Couldn't put it down, risk spilling it, or let anyone offer to take it from her.

'Have you got your invitation to the meeting, Goldilox?' Sadna asked.

'Yes, it's in the Klinnkwik girls' locker. Have you got yours?'

'Yes, but I haven't bought food for the evening meal so somewhere along the way, I've got to keep my eyes open, and buy something. Perhaps a cauliflower. Or maybe there'll be a fisherman at Grand River North West. But then, what would I do with a fish until tonight?'

'After the meeting we'll go and collect Giovanni from his after-school lessons. The Boy Who Won't Speak will already be at home. Will he be sewing, Jumila? And Sadna, your friend will have collected the twins from the crèche, so we can go past her house and pick them up too on our way home,' Goldilox said. Sadna had baby twins, 'the little boy' and 'the little girl', she called them.

'Come to my house after the party meeting and before we go to the party,' said Jumila. 'Perhaps we can cook together. I'm cooking dhall in a special way. My boss gave me this recipe. A legacy. Together with a weird poem. Bring your cauliflower to my house, we'll make a light curry with it and potato.'

'I'll bring sardines to make a chutney. Suit you? Let's get this job over with. Then we can get on with our day's activities. Just Jumila can be sad a while. Mourning the loss of. You will, Jumila. But probably only after we've got rid of it.'

The bus conductor recognized Jumila from a picture in the newspapers after the housing demonstration (she had been on page one), so he asked her how he could join the House Movement.

'Where do you live?' she asked him.

'Plenn Vert,' he said, 'but the landlord's got a court order for me to leave in six months. I've got three months left.'

'Free on Saturday? Yes? There'll be a meeting under the big mango tree at the top end of Magon Street. Four or so. You'll see the others gathering.'

'Where are you three going?'

65

'Grand River bridge,' said Jumila, anxiety creeping into her again.

'Six rupees,' he said.

When they got to the bridge, it was still raining.

But there *were* people on the bridge and everywhere around the bridge. Dozens and dozens of them. You could see them from inside the bus. What were they doing out in the rain?

Fishermen. There were fishermen everywhere. They were on the bridge, fishing over the edge. They were on both banks and on the islets in the middle of the river. Some of them were crowded into dubious *pirogues* fishing over the edge, all rods on the same side.

The *sisar* were on the run. Men and boys everywhere. At peace, fishing. In old clothes. Bicycles lying on the riverbanks. Dogs had come with some of them.

'Why don't they just all fish all the time,' said Sadna.

'What you mean?' asked Goldilox Soo.

'They look so nice, fishing,' said Sadna. 'I've never been fishing. Can we go fishing one day? The three of us, and Giovanni and The Boy Who Won't Speak. I can even bring the twins?'

They looked at the men and boys sitting quiet on overcrowded *pirogues*. No friction. Calm and silent. They realized there were hundreds of fishermen. None of them put off by the rain. Quietly waiting. Pulling in *sisar* one after the other. And even fishermen-watchers, on the bridge itself, with their umbrellas up, watching. Not critically, not competitively, but just there to see. To pay respect to fisher-men. Witnesses to the good in mankind.

'We don't want them witnessing us. And the fishermen themselves don't like interruptions. Never know what they'll think faced with a foetus. It might undermine them. Men don't know where all the miscarriages and abortions go. Let alone the spirits of the dead people. Some parts of real life are hidden behind a veil for men. A kind of purdah between their eyes and part of the world.'

'And what if they foul-hook it, or snag it, and pull up a foetus?' Jumila was worried. 'Like a man catching a mer-maid that runs after him, up to his house, and moves in.'

'I feel as though I foul-hooked it, and pulled it up myself. Even I don't know what to do with it? What would they do? The men? Would they just throw it back over the edge of the *pirogue* quietly? What if it floated? What if it followed their *pirogue*?'

So, they thought, we'll go under the bridge and look for a place where there aren't fishermen.

But even *there* there were fishermen.

Under the bridge, right there, were prostitutes as well, waiting for clients, knowing that even in this inclement weather, brothel clients being determined creatures, they would be there. So there had to be prostitutes, plying their trade. And men paired off in couples and in threes sniffing brown sugar off foil papers. As if having an affair with their own noses. 'They won't bother us,' Goldilox Soo said. But if they dwelt there, they would get 'Off my beat' comments

67

from the girls. Sure as hell. Especially being three women, and young. Or so said Sadna Joyna. 'Or the police will be along, and we'll be *guilty parties*, even surer than hell. They will start with the assumption that we're *"femmes de mœurs legères"* and do us for infanticide instead.'

This rain, in a sudden downpour that drove them back up on to the bridge and under the bus shelter, brought a wave of heat. Water everywhere, but they couldn't wash away the foetus. No way. It was stuck to them.

'It'll start rotting,' Sadna Joyna said in a whisper. Still only one green fly. Blue silver black green. It stuck like glue.

'By the way. Just out of curiosity, Jumila, was it going to be a boy or a girl? Do we know?' it was Sadna's turn to be curious, she didn't say *you*. She whispered the question, checking on the effect of the question on Jumila.

'Didn't look. Not sure I want to know.'

'How come you never told me?'

'Look, I'll show you both. I got a negative result at the chemist's test. See?'

She ferreted about in her bra and brought out a slip of paper, proof and all.

Before this, she hadn't really looked at it. She had seen just one word. Just the word *negative*. And then as she opened it to show them, she began, for the first time, to see, to see that there was some mistake.

'Oh, there's been a mistake. I'm a fool.'

It didn't say Jumila Goomann, but Jayamani Goodann, and a different address, not Jumila's, and the word *negative*.

'Look,' she said. 'Look.'

Some realizations are too heavy.

They take time.

They cause short circuits and confusion. They feel like some trick. Some twist of destiny. There is something they have to take note of. Fast. There is something terrible. But not one of the three women can place it in the first seconds, as they begin to realize what the mistake means.

'She'll have got one saying Jumila Goomann and the word *positive* on it,' Sadna says. 'She might also not read it properly. She might get such a fright from the word *positive*. Oh, Jesus. We'll have to find her. What if she goes and has one when she isn't even pregnant? Risks her life for nothing. How long ago did you have this test?'

'Look at the date on it. Just four weeks ago,' said Jumila.

'Oh, no,' said Goldilox Soo.

'There may still be time,' said Jumila, thinking. 'She may have tried *latizann* from the bazaar first, and then drinking other poisonous concoctions. She may have tried throwing herself down on a concrete pathway. Or maybe she's got rid of it, and everything's fine now. But what if she is about to have one? About to go and see Mama Naga or someone? For nothing? It's possible. It's unlikely. But we have to go and warn her, just in case.' None of them thought she may have *wanted* to be pregnant.

'Let's go look for her,' Sadna said.

'But we haven't got rid of the foetus yet,' said Goldilox Soo.

69

'Don't I know it,' said Jumila, 'but the alive and the living come first. Jayamani must be found.'

'One thing I can suggest is I know the driver of the offal lorry that comes to the hospital in the night. He will be there at about eleven,' Sadna suggested. 'A fall back plan. Contingency.'

'In the meantime what can we do with it?' Jumila asked, beginning to feel like a fisherman who has foul-hooked a mermaid.

'We've got no choice. We have to go and see her. In case she gets an abortion done for nothing, some badly-done backstreet abortion, and gets the bleeding, or the fever, or the gangrene, and dies?'

Three women who had one problem are now four women with two problems. But the second problem is more urgent than the first. Mortal.

And the fourth woman doesn't even know she hasn't got a problem. Or didn't have one. If only they could be in time. If only they could arrive in time.

'That's the trouble with women, when we haven't got a problem, we don't know it.' That was Goldilox Soo. 'No one usually bothers to even tell us. Let's see that address. I've got bus-fare money, if we have to go far,' says Goldilox Soo.

'Oh, 23 Mozart Avenue, Sité Valiji. It's on our way. That means we *have* to go. I know the street. My twin brother and I used to live near there. That means we must go and see her.'

'When things are illegal, the secretiveness itself leads to other things,' mused Jumila. 'Oh, no.'

'Are you managing, Jumila?' said Sadna.

'Of course,' she said. 'Of course.'

'I've got time before my case,' said Sadna, 'I'm coming too.'

Unsuspecting, Sadna Joyna had been that evening. The laces of her red ballet shoes were tied over her shoulders with the red shoes swinging here and there when she, a young lass at the time, came home into the alley where she and her mother Queen Victoria lived with the dog Sheeba with seven pairs of tits with shaggy hair on them and their two crates full of bananas and their cardboard boxes with Cape Apples written on them full of bananas and their wheelbarrow of bananas that the dog Sheeba was tied to, one evening, it was a Wednesday after dancing classes at the *L'Alliance Française*, going into their alley – the alley behind the Semino, you know that café where the prostitutes held the pimps to ransom one morning at about half-past ten when the sun already slanted into taxi drivers' eyes and under bus drivers' caps making each put one hand up so they could see potential passengers but which was the prostitutes starting-work time, and one of them announced that the broken beer bottles at throats was about income sharing, yes they knew big words, they knew that kind of concept, income sharing, and they each held a beer bottle in their right hand for the right-handed and in her left hand for the left-handed one, by the bottleneck, like a handle, and they broke the bottles in half in unison in one cymbal sound on the edge of the nearest café table as if there was a great conductor somewhere in the universe organizing orchestras like this one and they each held the jagged edge to a pimp's throat, which was at least a three-to-one ratio and stood there on this diamond-studded Semino floor and waited for negotiations to get underway, and naturally the clients fled at the cymbal sound itself, clients, mind-you, so stubborn they came out the minute a Class Three cyclone warning was taken off, making the girls have to get back on the beat at once as if they were electricity workers or some other essential service sectors, but clients shy of scandal and policemen and public denunciations, and even the phlegmatic taxi drivers all inched their cars forward a few yards towards the exit to get their windscreens out of the way and cleared their throats as well as their cars' throats, while not seeming to actually run away from a few loose women with jagged beer bottles, because you never know with enraged women, and these women were enraged with decades of rage, rage that started when the Semino opened its doors when the railways were first built and that went right through to the closing down of the railways and on even afterwards when just this word Semino was left to remind us of the train station, the word left on a noisy café at the

Victoria Station which station was now reduced to being a mere bus station, that much rage they had, and the two policemen going past went just that much faster past, when they saw what was going on because they weren't stupid when it came to judging how much rage – that alley.

She and her mother and the dog Sheeba lived in that alley. They had to put their bedding, their clothing, their cooking things and their supplies in a cupboard every morning in the alleyway, but the whole alleyway was theirs from six p.m. to six a.m. And it was home. There were mosquitoes and fruit flies and cockroaches and rats. But it was home. Warm as a womb. Happy as a bird's nest. And it regenerated the Queen and her daughter Sadna Joyna every day. The Queen paid for the dancing lessons twice a week but she sent Sadna there every afternoon to keep her off the streets. The Queen was very repetitive about this 'keep you off the streets'. Until we can be together in the alley at six.

But that evening that alley was all wrong.

Their alley was not right.

Even before she got there she knew.

She heard a silence from just outside it. She noticed it just as she leaned towards the crooked tin door before opening it. The door to the alley they lived in was too quiet. She put her ear to it and didn't hear her mother Queen Victoria singing while she cooked on the charcoal burner. She didn't hear the sound of dhall cooking in the

73

pressure cooker. She didn't hear anything she should have heard. She waited.

The silence persisted and signed its name. Death. No, it can't be.

She put her nose into the air and sniffed. She smelt a smell of Sheeba-fear in the air, even before she opened the door. Yes it is.

And then she smelt the smell of urine. Dead urine.

The smell signed a death warrant or a death certificate. Sadna Joyna knew.

She knew she would be on her own now. A world without her mother. Her loony mother, the only person she had, would be gone. The emptiness was already heavy and dark and obliterating.

She knew it was a crime. Not just a death. Death by crime. By somebody's hand. You could smell it.

And her mother's irritating words came into her mind: 'Go see Mrs Blignault. If anything happens to. Good woman. Work in her house. Until she gets you a job in government. Sweeping a social centre. Or as hospital servant.'

She leaned closer, hoping it was a moment of silence, for no reason at all, an ordinary moment of silence holding no foreboding. That she had just imagined it all.

But no, she was right. There was nothing. The breathing had stopped.

Or, maybe, her mother had just gone out for a minute. Try to think of something else. Out to fetch a box of matches.

But inside of her, she knew she wouldn't leave the bananas. In any case, the smell of Sheeba-fear stank in her nostrils.

'Sheeba,' she called, scared to open the tin door.

'Sheeba!' No sound of her tail wagging against the cardboard box.

It was certain.

She suddenly saw a tomorrow yawning ahead. A tomorrow without her mother wheeling the barrow with the dog Sheeba tied to it to the middle of the Victoria Station. Without her setting up her throne on an upside-down crate. Without her setting up in front of her the other upside-down crate and three upside-down cardboard boxes all with the bananas so beautifully arranged tourists would take her picture.

She knew it. Just below her elbow ached with sorrow. Queen Victoria was dead. Long live the Queen.

She knew she would be the one to discover the crime. First on the scene of the.

Woman of no fixed abode found dead. Foul play suspected.

She breathed in, summoned courage. Pushed on the tin door, opened it, and saw the dead Sheeba, expression of fear petrified on her open, blank eyes. Seven pairs of tits forever dry.

And behind the banana crates, her mother. Strangled with her own flimsy old sari. The Queen is dead.

Reclining on a cardboard box, a serene smile, the same

one she always had when she sat on her throne, was still there. Forever.

There's no two people so close on this earth as a loony mother and her only daughter.

Sadna Joyna went up to the Queen and touched her forehead. Already cold and dry. She kissed her, then drew away. She was broken in half.

Half of her lay there smiling with her *horni* strangling her. Bananas all around her. A tourist could almost take a picture.

The other half of her took the red ballet shoes from around her neck and without so much as looking at them, stuffed them into the drum beside the rubbish from the Semino. As she shoved them into the corner of the drum, she realized there were flies on a transparent plastic bag and when she looked closer even in that half-dark she thought she saw a bloodied foetus. Maybe, had it only become life, the Queen's spirit might have moved in. The Queen's thoughts were already starting to move into Sadna Joyna. Red ballet shoes gone. She only danced for the Queen. And the Queen was dead now.

Line Barracks was just around the corner. So she reported the crime and spent all night giving statements and depositions and going to the scene of the crime with the police doctors and police photographers. And they took her mother's body off to the Civil Hospital morgue for a post-mortem and the dog Sheeba's too. Some vet would cut Sheeba open, and maybe in passing marvel at the seven pairs of hairy tits never to feed a litter again.

Certainly the state took more note of the Queen and Sheeba after their deaths than during their lives. Must have spent a packet on them. She realized that this thought was her mother's.

She stopped school as well as dancing. In fact, she stopped, full stop.

That's what it felt like.

Stopping. Full stop.

It wasn't just that there was no money, so she had to stop school and look for work; nor was it just that she didn't have a house and had to look for a job with a room thrown in. It wasn't even the stopping dancing. Because you could dance in your head, she soon found out. It wasn't just that the dog Sheeba with the seven pairs of hairy tits got killed the same night, and this made her get muddled as to whether her mother was a wolf, or the dog a mother.

It was all these things as well.

But with the Queen gone, life itself lost its lustre. Its soul slipped off with the Queen and Sheeba. Slunk off and went and hid somewhere just out of reach.

Every rupee looked dull, when it didn't come in exchange for four bananas sold by the Queen. Every person in the country lost a certain aura when he or she was no longer a potential banana customer, but just a passer-by. Bus conductors were no longer people who could keep an eye on your bananas while you went for a pee in the smelly public lavatories at the end of the veranda, but just ordinary bus conductors. Taxi drivers were no longer individual acquaintances who knew you as the daughter of Queen Victoria but people touting for clients. New dhall puri sellers came and didn't even recognize you when you went past as though you were a nobody. Only Maraz and his son remembered you, and without looking up from the curry they put into the *faratas* they gave you free, with the chilli sauce on top, they said, father like son, 'Still miss the old girl? Long live the Queen!' and sometimes added, 'An unsung heroine. Well, life goes on.'

But life didn't go on.

It stopped, and then slowly started again, grey and dingy, full of hypocrite strangers and obsequious acquaintances. Joe and Tiraj, the pickpocket brothers, instead of being clever and witty and wise, seemed mean and sordid. And the prostitutes of the Semino went on accepting a bad deal from half-past ten in the morning till all hours without ever raising broken beer bottles again.

All because the Queen was dead.

No one actually took her place, nor the place of her bananas under the Victoria Station carved into the rock building. But merchants encroached – one who sold strings to hold glasses around your neck, and another who sold mealie pudding. But there were no bananas anymore. No throne. No Queen. If you go and stand and look at the Victoria Bus Station in Porlwi right now, this minute, you will see the place where her throne was, where she sat in waiting. The space is still there.

They said that technically Sadna could apply for a place in a girls' home, as an abandoned minor, but that practically it would be difficult due to so many girls getting 'beyond control' orders slapped on them and filling the homes up.

She said she had family. They said who. She said they lived in Pudor. Not to worry she had money for the bus.

She had money. Her mother kept it behind a loose stone in the old wall of the alley. It was still there. Whatever they killed her and Sheeba for, they didn't get the money. Four thousand rupees. All made from bananas. In her bank account as well, there was the same amount again. But she wouldn't be able to draw it until she was eighteen so she kept it a secret and hid her State Bank book in her flat bra.

So she went to look for Mrs Blignault like her mother had said she should. 'If anything ever happens to me,' she had said, laughingly, 'there's the loose stone in the wall, there's the State Bank account, and then there's Mrs Blignault who lives in a big concrete house in Ward Kat. Number 23 *bis* in Bancillon Street. You do her housework for her. And get her to get you a job in government.'

The reason she went was she couldn't think of anything else to do. So she caught a tip-top bus to the end of Mrs Street, almost thinking it might be named after Mrs Blignault. And walked up and down until she found number 23 *bis*.

It was like a crooked castle. She shuddered. A prison. After the freedom of the alley, what was this going to be? The gate had a lock on it. She must be out, she thought.

But she saw a shadow by the upstairs window. It looked and then it peered. Behind a curtain.

She called, 'Mrs Blignault!'

And there she was, struggling with the lock.

She was relieved that Mrs Blignault had the key to her prison.

She opened it, said, 'Come in. I was expecting you. Cyril said the CID told him that your mother and her dog had been killed. And I remembered my promise and so you see I knew you would be here. I've told Cyril. I've said you'll be on my doorstep soon. My condolences. I loved your mother.'

She hugged Sadna.

'Don't worry. You can stay. He's agreed to give you the second garage. There's an outside toilet. And two hundred rupees for being *bonne à tout faire*. And maybe you could teach me to dance.'

Sadna asked her why she was having her to stay and work without any questions.

'It's an old story. Perhaps I'll tell you one day. Perhaps I won't.'

So Sadna Joyna got a job and a place to stay. And Mrs Blignault promised to prepare her first application to work as a hospital servant as soon as she turned eighteen. 'It's what I promised your mother I'd do. But we must go and do some painting. There are one or two things I've been longing to paint, but I didn't have anyone to come with me.'

Then she went on.

'I don't go out much. He doesn't let me. He doesn't even let me go to mass. Not that that's the worst of it, but you wouldn't think he would have the cheek to stop me going to church. But he does. Maybe if you come with me, he'll let me. Will you?'

'Of course,' said Sadna Joyna. 'No objection.'

'No, she's not here. She's, um, she's at work. At the factory. Why? What's she to you three?' He had come out of the door and was standing on the bright red, slippery polished pathway to the front gate, where the three of them waited. He had heard women's voices calling, 'Jayamani, Jayamani!' He was scared to walk on the red polished path because the rain had made it too slippery. She was a good housewife. Her garden had roses, pruned. There was a tiny lawn, with an elf statue in it. One hand broken. And one windowpane missing in the only window facing the road, the small sité house window. Contradictory path and window. A child peeped around the edge of the house and vanished. Squawked. Then vanished.

'She's a friend of a friend of ours. You know, an acquaintance.'

'What do you want with her?' He was cross.

'Just a message.'

'Leave it with me. I'm her husband. Have you got a parcel for her?' Innocent question.

'No, no, no.' Goldilox Soo put the plastic bag behind her back. Don't want to look guilty either. 'They said to give her the message in person. Just a message. It isn't bad news or anything. What time will she be back?' and trying her luck Goldilox Soo added, 'What factory does she work at then?'

'The button factory. In Plenn Lozan.'

When they started to set off, as if to the button factory, her husband called after them.

'Wait a minute. I lied. She's here. At home. I'm off work to look after her. I lied. What is it? I don't understand anything anymore. Talk to her a while. You're not from police or probation or anything like that are you? She's sick. Don't know what she's had. She's over it now. But look at her. Hospital saved her life. She was on the kidney machine.'

When they went in, there she was, sitting on the back landing, on a broken rattanware chair, doubled over in illness of some sort. As though she, too, like the chair, was broken.

The child squawked again and ran off again.

'I'll take him to Lasalinn to the swings while your friends are here,' the husband said. He checked that this seemed reasonable. Ran after the child, caught him by the hand, and dragged him off kicking, but pleased.

'When I got the positive test I panicked what with the child I've got being handicapped if you watch him in a minute when they get back you'll see he's like a monkey quite bats and he never does anything bad on purpose never he's a happy child it's just me that has to watch him watch over him never take my eyes off of him and there I was so disbelieving when I saw the results and the panic because I hadn't missed a single pill and I only had the test because I'd had this nightmare terrible nightmare makes me shudder this nightmare about having two more like him and them running wild all three two girls and a boy and stealing and running away and annoying people and getting on to aeroplanes at Plezans Airport and none of them doing it on purpose they were just such happy springy lively creatures and I loved them all three like I love him but I was getting tired in this nightmare so tired I couldn't lift my feet and they dragged on the ground and then they felt like the ground was turning into a marsh and my feet wouldn't move forwards and I woke up terrified that I was pregnant and pregnant with twin monkey girls because on his own he's already so full of energy and breaks things and screams and runs around and the doctors say he's got the mind of a four-year-old but I find him very clever like as I say a monkey not in the bad sense just naughty and I love him and he's quite dangerous off hitchhiking and he's only nine and climbing on top of people's houses and squawking if ever he gets out and pulling the curtains down and pouring the rice-grains and lentils on to the floor no harm meant just to play and begging from neighbours and turning taps on and overflowing the washbasin on purpose yes that's it he just plays but for the mother for the mother oh my god for the mother so I spoke to my husband told him about the positive test and he agreed lord knows he knows my suffering with just this one and he's a good man taken a day off today to help me with him he's even done the pathway you know polished it and yes he agreed about the getting rid of it which is why he's so upset now because he says he shouldn't have agreed what if the priests are right and god is punishing us he's a bit religious you know and even superstitious but that doesn't help and I would have done it anyway behind his back I can tell you that and I was quite prepared to die I was resigned to that risk but somehow not this one not this now I can't walk anymore I didn't expect this anyway when he agreed I went to see this nurse well they say she's a nurse on Laburdone Street he came with me otherwise they wouldn't do it you have to be accompanied two hundred and fifty rupees plus thirty rupees downpayment on the catheter thing they put in which you have to return which I haven't it's in my handbag do you think I ought to return it but then afterwards I got so sick with the fever and he took me to the hospital he said you'll die if I don't take you and the doctors were very nice to me they saw I was in a bad way they put me in the slip-and-fall ward then they said it was already septicaemia then they said my kidneys were in temporary failure so I had to have dialysis but the government machine was broken down so the government paid for me to go to this clinic the Catholic sisters' one in Reduit and everyone thought I would die the doctors the sisters muttering to my husband and the hospital doctors came to the clinic and there were specialists and in my dreams I heard a woman I don't know who she was but she was shouting at doctors and sisters and saying that the law was killing women and no policeman would question a woman on her death bed in her ward and I said goodbye to the earth and to my little monkey child and everything went black and I think I died but then no I turned around and came back and when I came back I had had this septic arthritis and I'm crippled see how I walk all doubled over like an old lady my knees don't bend or unbend much they just stay like this and nor do my elbows so the government ambulance takes me for heat treatment and for some physiotherapy and they say I might get some movement back all depends how much damage is already done and what are you doing here you three you look very nice I'm sorry I can't receive you better why do you listen to me what's in your plastic bag I can see on your faces there's something wrong there's trouble in the plastic bag isn't there and I seem to recognize one of you.'

'Yes trouble. Oh trouble. More trouble. How much more trouble can we stand.' It was Goldilox Soo. Jumila couldn't speak. She felt sick. She felt like The Boy Who Won't Speak. She felt she could give up speaking forever. She took the plastic bag from Goldilox Soo and held it close to her. Only now did she embrace it as hers. Only now would she be able to part with it. She felt maybe it hadn't been a practical

85

problem at all, not being able to get rid of it, but that she had been attached to it. After all, she could have just stuffed it into any rubbish bin. But perhaps she hadn't been ready yet. None of them had been ready.

Then she gave it back to Goldilox Soo.

She went over to the woman, the new strange woman who spoke in one sentence, and would not be shining her own front path any more.

She picked her up out of her chair, to stand, inasmuch as she could stand. And she hugged her, hugged her, and cried on her shoulder. Mourning for the living.

'Jayamani,' was all that Jumila could say.

'Are you crying for me?' she asked.

'Yes,' said Jumila.

Then Jumila said, 'It should have been me.' She took out the folded bit of paper. Then she said. 'I don't suppose you want to look in the bag. I haven't. It came down by itself. I didn't know I was pregnant. It doesn't matter anymore. It's all over now. You have suffered all this for nothing. That's what happens when we, you and me, have to skulk around.

'And we didn't get here in time. I also didn't look at my results properly until today, today when all this mess came down and I don't know how to get rid of it.'

The mad little boy pounced down through the open window, he and his father had got back all of a sudden, and he grabbed the plastic bag from Goldilox Soo and looked into it.

86

He got scared and started saying, 'Hot, hot, hot,' which was the word he knew for dangerous things. It could burn you, he was warning.

Quite right.

He and his father were back from the park. His father's patience was short.

'I saw you that first day, when you were on Ward Eleven,' said Sadna Joyna. 'That's why you recognize me. If only I had known.'

'What could anyone have known?' Jayamani said.

'I'm a collector, Jumila,' said the historian's wife, Jumila's new boss, 'and I collect three things: my own poems, though I throw most of them away. I also collect the best recipes, which implies throwing away most of those too. I also collect ideologically loaded statements but there are so many these days, masquerading as fact, that my collection is too big. Do you know what those are?'

'Recipes, yes. Poems, maybe. Ideologically loaded statements, no,' said Jumila. 'But what's this got to do with me working here, Madam?'

'Nothing whatsoever. What so ever. Call me Liz. I may just give some item to you from time to time for you to look at. I need someone to show my things to sometimes. You'll do just fine. I get scared at night. Not scared of anything. Just scared of my own thoughts. I just want to know you're there. There. There, with The Boy Who Won't Speak. Then I won't feel so lonely. Do you understand?

'I don't ever want to see you working in my house though.' She went on with her soliloquy. 'You can come in whenever you want to, and work any time so long as I'm out. I don't want to feel I've got a servant. You work in the house only when I'm at work, or out somewhere else. When I get back, no work. Most of the time you can just leave me alone. And for god's sake don't let me see you doing my housework. But as for The Boy Who Won't Speak, do you mind if I call him in sometimes, to keep me company. Consider me your babysitter in this respect. You can go out and leave him, and tell me what time to expect you back home. And never, never call me Madam again.'

'Home?'

'Yes, you can have the little flat at the back. Do you want to see it before you decide?'

Bliss, she thought.

Jumila had found her boss by chance. Her mother's sister washed clothes at a woman's house, and this woman was a colleague of the historian's wife. They both taught at the Loretto Convent. She had said the historian's wife needed a live-in woman domestic employee. Jumila had noted this, and went to her house to look for work.

Seemed like a funny job, this one.

Jumila had been sure she wouldn't take her once she heard about The Boy Who Won't Speak. But that seemed to be why she took her on. Because of him. She asked a lot about him, and about his dead mother, who she said she had known, and was all quiet and thoughtful and said, 'Yes, I like you, Jumila.'

Then Jumila said, 'I hope my ex-husband doesn't come and make trouble. He may.' And the historian's wife said, 'Don't worry, what trouble can he make here? If you want to kick him out, kick him out. I'm with you on that one. Trouble is only if you're embarrassed. I'm not. Sometimes I think I would be better kicked out. But of course he would never do me that favour. He would never kick me out. He's too nice. A historian, you know, my husband. And very nice. Everyone says so.'

'Or my big brother, the religious one, he might also come and make trouble.'

'That need not be a worry of yours.'

She was an imaginative woman.

She worked as an economics teacher and wrote witty articles for the newspaper. Jumila had read them once or twice. Rahim liked reading them. She didn't tell Liz she'd read any of her articles.

'I send Rs100 to the Women's Movement every month by a stop order,' she told Jumila. 'But don't ask me to go to meetings, I told them. I'm busy writing and collecting things. It's the same with you. You can work here, but don't expect to get any instructions or anything. Just your pay. And I'll show you the odd item from my collections, and call in the boy. Understand?'

The flat at the back was perfect.

89

The first and last recipe she sent to Jumila she left on the kitchen table. The historian never came into the kitchen himself, so Jumila knew it must be for her. In any case she was expecting it. It read as follows:

DHALL

Take equal parts of yellow dhall, red lentils and black lentils (the latter can be the broad ones or the small ones) and boil up with salt until soft. Pressure cooker or microwave quicker. While this is going on, you put your mind to browning the onions in a separate little cooking pot. Now, here is the important part: for dhall or lentils, or this mixture of both, onions must not only be browned in oil, but slowly, slowly, slowly, over a low heat OVER-browned. But not blacked. When browned to the over-browning point, take them off the fire and add the crushed garlic and the thyme (fresh if poss.). Then put a couple of spoons of garam masala (which hasn't got turmeric in it) and stir it into the oil over a low heat, for a minute or two, till it smells cooked and not yet burnt. (It'll be bitter if not cooked in oil, and it'll be bitter if over-cooked in the oil.)
Then add to the big pot. It makes a sizzling sound, which is the reward for the cooking.
Then you take a half a cup of yoghurt and add the lentil soup to it slowly until it is creamy, emulsified.

(If you add the yogurt to the soup without doing
this first, it stays in lumps.)
Add curry leaves.
Then add salt to taste.
Serve in a bowl, that can be poured over each
person's rice at will.

Jumila took note of three different things: mixing different
kinds of pulse, and using yoghurt instead of tamarind,
garam masala instead of turmeric.

Soon the historian's wife asked The Boy Who Won't
Speak if she could read her stories to him. That was a new
thing: her stories. They were made-up stories, written
down, and Jumila didn't know what was in them. She
thought they were made up just for The Boy Who Won't
Speak. It was one of the only things The Boy Who Won't
Speak liked. And she would let him watch her sewing. The
historian's wife noticed that when he sat still and watched
her sewing on her Singer hand sewing-machine, the
haunted look in his eyes would abate somewhat. So she
gave it to him. She bought herself a new electric one, and
said Jumila, have this, for The Boy Who Won't Speak, when
she gave Jumila her first month's pay.

And then the historian's wife taught him to sew. And
that's what he does. He sews. And he brings in some
money. Now in the squatter's tin shack on the mountain
flank. Only it's terrible to see him sitting on a chair and
sewing on their bed, leaning over like that, in the dark

shack. But he loves sewing. With the practice at people's sizes from selling bras, he can sew clothes for people without measuring them up.

She gave Jumila the following poem that she wrote:

Sea Change

The drugged midday breathing
Of sleeping beasts swarmed under the trees.
People – puppets between the shows –
Lolled in the shade of rocks (No one
Was out in that sun) and hung
About in the shade of palms, lasting.
Slackened between two worlds, they wait
For their old
And their sick
To stop breathing to die.
The sea retreated,
Sacrificing its own body to the sun.
Damp rose in the air, unable to muster
A cloud, only this smother.
On such a day
She enters.
She kneels on hot sand,
On that deserted beach.
(Blowlamp removes her brain.
Heat bends air. All loses
Solidity and form. All

Becomes a mirage.)
Strikes the match.
(No flame, nor little world around it –
The sun sees to that)
Sulphur tip merely blackens
And blackness, like a creeping realization,
Led by a jagged blade
Spreads up the pale match.
Into a thin sprinkling of ashes.
Watches prose,
Even verse,
Turn into mirage,
Go to sand,
Join its own shadow.
The sun went down
The tide rose up
Over the heap of sand
In which she had buried her ashes.

Jumila didn't understand it. But liked it nevertheless. That's the case with poems sometimes. But it made her scared. No, not exactly scared. Uneasy. Worried. As if her boss held her own ashes in her hands.

But she never gave Jumila a single one of her collection of ideologically loaded statements. She left Jumila as a legacy the desire to know what she meant by this. Maybe, she thought, it was some kind of a private joke. Jumila never found out.

Anyway, she, Jumila's boss, started to cry a lot. Jumila could see her in the morning through the window.

And one day, she just sat down in the kitchen next to Jumila and The Boy Who Won't Speak. 'Stay, I have something to say.'

She said, 'You know all this despising I've had from him, it's nothing. Husbands often do it. I'm used to it. And from his family too. The ongoing meaning transmitted to me and reinforced every day, that I'm not good enough. Why didn't I marry someone where I came from if I was any good. That shows how hard up I am that I marry their son and brother. And they tell me not to be friends with these people, they're too dark, nor with those, they're too pale to meet us. And if only he had married someone else. I take all this as normal now. Though no one else should. And this is what finally makes me feel sad. My having accepted is nothing, for me. I even thought it was courageous of me. Brave historian's wife. Putting up with so much. At worst I thought I didn't count. But what is the meaning for other people, for people who come after me, of my having accepted, having bowed down, having given up like that? I hadn't ever realized I was being nasty to other people by putting up with things, by bowing down to things, by grinning and bearing things. It never dawned on me. Shows how self-centred I was, or am.

'I too have created and recreated every day and still create and recreate every day this web of categories, of mindless divisions which insult myself and you and every human on this earth. By allowing this to go on, I have done it.

'And now you see. Now there's something else. It's my children. Both of them. The boy and the girl. They look at everyone like that too. I never showed them otherwise. They even look at me like that. Me. They see me, the same as he does, and all his family. Well naturally. I never opposed it. They classify. I mean by ethnic origin, by so-called culture, by ancestral religion, by invented past language spoken, by passport, by colour, by hair, by nail and tooth. I am a dog, bred and inbred and outbred, not a person. I am reduced to being a bitch. I never ought to have colluded with this. Those too pale, those too dark. Those white, those black. Those Hindu those Muslim. Those Tamil. Those Chinese. Those too good for us. Those not good enough. Now I am like that, Jumila. Now I am seen by the young, innocent ones like that. Now I am left all alone. And it's my own fault. I am evil, Jumila. If I had met The Boy Who Won't Speak earlier, maybe he could have taught me courage.'

'Children, Madam?'

'Oh, you didn't even know. You see, I've blotted them out, in a way. I can hardly believe what they're like. Yes. I've got two children. We've got. They'll be back for school holidays today. They're at university abroad. I don't think I can bear it.'

'What? Your children will be here, Madam,' Jumila said. 'You should be pleased. This is a blessing.'

'Is this,' Liz asked, 'what happened to your mother?' She

95

looked at The Boy Who Won't Speak. 'She was a lovely woman, your sister,' she said to Jumila. And The Boy Who Won't Speak smiled. 'Did she,' she went on, 'find out that she had lived lies too long? Even when they were over from the outside, when that man was gone, the lies were still there, inside her?

'I should have got myself hence to a nunnery.'

'How was it you knew her?' asked Jumila.

'I'm sorry.'

They didn't know what she was sorry about. Jumila thought it was about her sister's death, about her suicide.

'I'm sorry. I'm only sorry because of you and The Boy Who Won't Speak. I'd like you to esteem me. For everyone else, my accepting has been bad. I regret that. But for you two it's much more important. I'm sorry.'

And it was that night that they found her. Her husband, son and daughter found her, in the bathroom, lying in blood, black blood, the last of it pulsing weakly from her two slit wrists red.

A red line pulls black
Over the page, which hovers
And then shivers.

Steel razor blades swam in the blood. When they got in from the airport. She had said she wouldn't come to the airport. Had a headache.

It stayed something of a mystery as to why she actually killed herself. Or how she had known The Boy Who Won't Speak's mother.

So The Boy Who Won't Speak lost another mother. No wonder she was sorry.

Jumila lost her boss. Her job. And her house.

And she was left as prey for her family. They had been waiting for such a moment. Her limp would get worse.

'I will not accept,' said Jumila, and The Boy Who Won't Speak smiled a wan smile of agreement.

And so they ended up in Kan Yolof, the place where all the dispossessed washed up, the place that is no place, just a place between other places.

At the Sité Valiji bus station, Jayamani was uppermost in their minds.

Sadna Joyna still saw her admitted feverish to Ward Eleven. Then saw her as she is now. The stiff knees and the bent back, etched into, engraved on to, Sadna's mind. Like a vision. Sadna's usual indignation, her usual bounciness, gave way to a wispy, hurt little girl's face.

She had just come across this mental image. It was just lying there in her mind. As if already there before she thought of it. It upset her. Jayamani's red ballet shoes had been ripped off her feet and were being burnt in front of

97

them both. They were forced to just watch and not do any-thing. Then the image started to become a narrative.

She saw Jayamani being put into head-shackles and leg-irons by some enslaving intruder. *Weapons for torturing slaves were still the practice in Mauritius long after being out-lawed elsewhere.* How did she know this? Was it the Queen who had told her? Yes. How did *she* know?

Leg-irons and neck-irons and shackles and balls-and-chains, she had said.

The Queen had taken her down under a bridge in Tranquebar, where on a ledge someone had hidden a neck-shackle. Someone wanting proof to live on? Who knows?

And now the tools of backstreet abortionists persist. Still the practice. She laughed to herself. The bishop has just last year asked forgiveness for the church's sins over slavery. She had heard the priest say so when she went to church with Mrs Blignault. The bishop's predecessors owned slaves, Mrs Blignault had told her. Like their buildings and their cars. Like their schools and their convents. Like real estate. Apologies, if there are to be any, will be too late for Jayamani, Sadna thought.

Jayamani had not submitted to her womb. Nor had she succeeded in killing herself. She was pinioned in-between the two. Half submitted, half killed herself.

The plastic bag within a plastic bag within a plastic bag just dangling limp in Sadna Joyna's hand now. Never born. Therefore never dead. Jayamani. Living. Surviving. The living always superseded the potential living, even if not the dead. Her monkey child, surviving.

She held up the bag now, Sadna did, made it dangle like a means of insulting some authority: 'You know what I think we should do with it. You know what I've got a good mind to do with it. Take it to Line Barracks, put it on the counter, and ask those policemen there to call the CID and put a case against us. Tell them to arrest poor Jumila and me, for example. Tell them to arrest us. We've got our witness, you Goldilox Soo. Let's make this public. We can't let this go on. Too much silence is a bad thing. Too much getting on with it. Look at the cost.'

'That's a good idea.' Jumila was smarting with the pain that could have been hers. 'But I feel a bit weak right now.'

'How many more women do they want to die? Why do we have to die like flies, and get crippled and all?' Sadna Joyna felt rage rise in her, descend on her, at the Sité Valiji bus station. She shared it with the other two.

Men stepped away from them. With an instinct for avoiding this kind of subject matter.

'Or go and leave it at the priest's house. In person. Ask to see him in person. Request a special service for departing foetuses. They say they're lives. Ask him to check if it's a boy or girl and baptise it. Ask him to get rid of it, while he's about it.' It was still Sadna speaking, now repeating what she had said sarcastically earlier at the hospital, in all earnestness now.

'There's a limit,' Sadna went on. 'And I've reached mine. That slip-and-fall ward, Ward Eleven, is enough.

'One day, you know what happened, I heard this in the women's meeting I went to last month. The bishop held this public conference at St Mary's hall. Public. Everyone invited. By poster. In the press. There were all the politicians and the journalists and the professionals and the uppercrust of Bobasin and Rozil. Against abortion.

'So they went, too. Members of the women's association went. They gave out leaflets. *Women are not rabbits. Nor are we incubators.* Things like that. They caused a stir.'

'Here's the bus,' said Goldilox Soo.

'Then what happened?' asked Jumila. 'What stir?'

They stood in a queue for a bus heading for Line Barracks. They looked at the bag. They put their arms near Jumila. Just in case. She still looked weak.

'Still OK?'

'Yes. Let's go to Line Barracks. If someone had gone to Line Barracks long ago, maybe we would not be sneaking around like criminals today.'

But, of course, there was the ongoing business.

Business as usual.

Who would look after The Boy Who Won't Speak if Jumila was away a day or two in police cells? He's all on his own selling bras right now. Who would feed Giovanni tonight, if Goldilox Soo disappeared? Sadna had her court case. No postponing that. And as for her tiny twins, they could stay with her kind friend for an hour or two. But what then?

And the three women had to get to a *meeting*. Today. There was trouble brewing up in the country. They had to help stop it. But the plastic bag was here. A presence. How could they take on the State?

Sadna Joyna didn't even have time to finish the story about the public conference and the stir some women were causing in it. Until today she hasn't finished telling it.

The other people in the queue were too near.

The same sound can have so many meanings. When Goldilox Soo heard that hoot as Sara drove the car into the drive – a signal for the day to begin for real – a hot, hot day, in the old wooden house calm under the thick shade of four dark, dark green mango trees, when she heard that, it sounded like a symphony.

She saw Sara looking up at her, even while she was still coming out on to the veranda, hands on her hips. Sara's hennaed head relaxing down on to the steering wheel almost upside down, like a reflection, to look out the car window up at the golden haloed head looking down. Their eyes like ponds. Twin ponds reflecting in twin ponds.

She didn't have to say 'Help me with the gas, Goldilox Soo' because Goldilox Soo already knew where Sara had come from and was waiting for her. Of course, Sara needed the gas. But there was also the Bombay Sweets, the incense, the half-jack of gin, a new CD and maybe a few metres of silk to put around their shoulders.

Everything would have been just as expected, except that she hit the pot that a fern was in, as she drove in, looking up for Goldilox Soo. The pot broke almost in half, and the front bit fell on to the stone driveway – it was an imitation Greek urn thing. Was the fender of the car bent? Goldilox Soo bent over and looked at the car square on. She shrugged. Sara decided that it wasn't or it didn't matter. He never noticed such things and got back home too late at night anyway. So they turned the pot around so that the side with the missing half wasn't so obvious.

'It's nothing, a little accident,' said Goldilox Soo. But it wasn't nothing. It enhanced the feeling in the air that day, a scent of the fragility of life, a hint of the chances of death. But the feeling passed. And that of jasmine rose.

'It's in bloom. Smell that, Goldilox Soo,' Sara said. And they both pretended to swoon.

They walked together to the IN gate, tucking in wisps of hair on one another's heads, and each pulled one half of the gate closed and slid the bolt from one side into its sheath on the other. Then they went around the crescent drive to the OUT gate and each pulled one half closed and slid its bolt into its sheath too.

They were enveloped in a thick shade that hid a harsh sun.

Goldilox Soo could have picked up the full gas cylinder and swung it on to her right shoulder and walked up the front steps with it. But she didn't. They carried it up together. Her hands always got stronger when she did something with someone else. And laughing up the steps with it, knees weak with enjoyment by the time they reached the long, thin windowpanes that made up the front of the house, like a myriad of mirrors, all reflecting lots of Saras and lots of Goldilox Soos. More twins.

Sara's husband, the managing director of the Millers' Group of Companies, had employed Goldilox Soo to look after her. Yes, that's how he'd said it: 'To look after her.' He had put an advertisement in *L'Express* smalls: 'Wanted immediately in the Senn Mars area, someone who is more than a *bonne à tout faire*, a companion. To live in. Excellent pay and conditions. Preferably without children.' This advertisement drew Goldilox Soo and Giovanni out of the woods. Sara's husband took a liking to Giovanni. And as for Goldilox Soo, she was just what he needed.

'You're strong enough to carry her yellow gas cylinder, that's what I want.'

He told Goldilox Soo that Sara was an alcoholic. He paid Goldilox Soo to accompany her during the day, and to live in at night. Sara did the cooking and her three children all did the washing up. There was a cleaning woman twice a week, and a dhobi came and took the clothes for washing and brought them back ironed. Professional window-cleaners came once a month to do the veranda windows. So, Goldilox Soo didn't have much work to do. 'I don't want anyone to know she drinks,' he had said. He gave

103

money for the drink and the rest. 'And don't let the kids know she drinks either.' Giovanni had his own room, and was treated as one of the children. Like today. They would all be together, on an outing after school in the helicopter with Sara's husband. Sara's husband would go straight from work, pick all four of them up after lessons, and take them on the treat. 'See all the greenness from above, and the turquoise.'

Sara's husband didn't know Goldilox Soo and Giovanni didn't have birth certificates. But then again, maybe he wouldn't have minded. Hard to know what was in his head. So calm and quiet and to himself.

Sara knew he had a second wife though. 'Nothing you can do about it,' she said to Goldilox Soo. 'He's got children on that side too. The law allows it. He never says anything. A few years back when he said he wanted me to have another child, I could afford the joke "Go have it with some other woman", but now with the new law, of course, the joke's on me. Mind you, I'm glad he's out of my hair. Not that I agree with that law. Maybe I lack courage. I should have just upped and offed a few years back. Now it's too late.'

Of course, everyone knew Sara drank. Only they all pretended they didn't know. But she wasn't an alcoholic like he said. 'Not yet anyway,' Goldilox thought. 'Got to her just in time.' He didn't want her messing around with other *men* either, as he put it. She interpreted the emphasis on the *men*, as being an emphasis on the plural of the word. It didn't matter that much if it were only one man and very discreet, at that. Say, a visitor, who brought a video-cassette every day, to keep her occupied. But she wasn't interested. And another thing, he wanted her to eat no pork. Goldilox Soo and the children too. She didn't mind. Hadn't had money to buy meat with anyway.

So after connecting up the gas, they went into the lounge and flopped down in a big old rattanware chair each, waiting for their eyes to get used to the dark inside.

'I've brought soft cotton for each of us. It looked so much cooler than the silk. Let's make ourselves a home dress each. Right now. Do you like it? I bought the same for us both. Like twins.

'Scissors, pins, blue chalk, needles and thread, the machine on a dining-room chair!' She gave orders.

Goldilox Soo issued counter-orders: 'Light the joss stick, unpack the Bombay sweets and serve the coffee first.'

Sara got out the new CD. 'A morning raga,' she said and put it on.

'Measuring tape! And pen and paper,' Sara ordered.

The fact that they were alone was crucial. And the way they had seen that pot broken in half, like a soul opening up for a body to be freed. But then, there was also the dizzying perfume of the jasmine and now the incense that flared their nostrils and called for slow breathing and hedonism. And the piercing notes of that particular morning raga, with the sitar that could engorge any woman's breast and nipple and the tabla that made your womb throb. It said, 'Let there never be need of an evening, let alone an evening raga.' There was the heat outside, a lazy heat that cried out that time had stopped and that don't worry the sun would always be there. No hurry. This, coupled with the temperate, dark inside of the wooden house. Women remember the wombs they were in once, and the wombs they have felt filled. And the fact, strange fact, that the lounge was so inside. So very inside. It had no window or door that opened to the outside. There were three sets of doors that only gave on to the long veranda that protected it to the front, the kids' rooms opened off one by one to the one side, Sara's and her husband's to the other, and the lounge was lined by the long wide back corridor with two doors on to it, which in turn gave on to the doors to the kitchen, the ironing room and Goldilox Soo's bedroom. Maybe it started when they each put a Bombay sweet between one another's lips and the almond milk sugar coconut melted.

And of course there was the measuring-tape.

Two people alone together taking off their clothes can always be a happy prelude. And when the Porlwi breeze ran over their naked shoulders just as they were deciding whether to measure with their underclothes on or with their underclothes off, the decision seemed so difficult that they sighed and their breasts rose and fell.

'We'll measure with them on and with them off, both,' said Goldilox.

This was how they came to be kneeling on the Persian carpet facing one another, measuring the length of one another's arms, writing it down on the bit of paper, their legs in turn, although they weren't making trousers, their wrists, in case they made long sleeves, and for good measure their ankles, and wrote it all down, around one another's bra-pointed breasts, slowly with care, then naked waists, causing a slight jump of muscle, then pantied hips. Slipping the measuring-tape up and down, left and right, to get it into place. Noticing a fluff of hair each.

The incense rose, slightly more heady. The raga rang deeper into their flesh, without clothes to keep the sound out. And Sara held up the soft cotton against Goldilox Soo's neck and let it fall down to the carpet.

'I can't tell you what you look like,' she said. So Goldilox Soo took the other end of the cloth and held it up against Sara's neck, and said, 'I know now.'

There was no prudishness in them.

No hesitation.

The idea and the knowledge and the innocence came suddenly and to both of them.

Each turned out one tit for the other to see, mirror image. An offering. One in, one out. And each touched the other's breast just once, to show appreciation of the sight.

Then the ministrations started.

Passion in two pairs of eyes, rising calm. Still kneeling. Now two nipples touch and two bras and two breasts touch, as their lips move towards one another's. The ordinary parcelling of time and space was gone. Ancient aeons were measured in other ways.

By the taste of Bombay sweets as their tongues touched.

Sounds sealed inside. The word of an embrace. And by words, those wild representations of the world, like, 'I will suck on this breast of yours until the end of time.' It was Sara. And she started a slow gentle sucking, gentle sucking, gentle sucking. Instead of measuring. Instead of taking off underwear in order to measure for making clothes. Like mother and child. Adults in innocence. Goldilox Soo put her head right back and stood one foot up and took hold of Sara's breast with both hands to balance herself and started a slow gentle fondling, gentle fondling, gentle fondling, instead of writing down a measurement, instead of noting and tabulating and keeping count.

The CD stopped. They looked one another in the eye. It was over, the morning raga. It had counted its time and come to an end. Not so with love-making. Time melts and waxes and wanes expands and contracts.

The sound of the world with all its timing came in through their ears, like an exciting challenge to their bodies, momentarily separated by the thinnest film of air. The cars, as if wasting their time, going round and round uselessly on the surface of the globe, some purgatory to be served. The cathedral bells, measuring half-way through yet another godless day. The mosque calling men to submit to time and to knock their foreheads against the surface of the earth. Merchants crying their wares in the distance. And the mango branch creaking against the tin roof of the double garage. As things inside you get deeper and more intense, only external things measure time. And they recede again.

'I can only hear your heart and mine,' said Goldilox Soo. 'And I must show you what I feel in the only way I know how.' And she put her head down to Sara's bare breast. Before starting to suck, she said, 'Like a mirror.' But Sara's leg, instead of straightening out to steady her, wrapped itself around Goldilox Soo's waist, and pulled their cunts together, which made Goldilox Soo suck fiercer, and lift Sara's two legs around her waist.

And so it was that they were without their underwear, though planned in a different way and neither knew how. And they arranged the new cotton material between two rattanware chairs and made a house into which they crept and started, in earnest, to make love.

Neither had ever known lovemaking. Only sex. And one orgasm only made them want another. And another another. Until they had to put the cloth under them, because of the Persian carpet.

They should have known it was too good to be true.

They should have listened with one ear.

They should have predicted.

What might happen.

But then nothing had been planned. So how could they? And sometimes there's a will for things to go wrong. In the events themselves. Some lack of courage. Some structural inequality they pretended wasn't there. Some residual hand-lessness. It's only in stories that hands grow back completely.

Sara's husband decided to come home first. Before going on the helicopter outing.

Something he never did, that, change his plans. He was a man who kept to his plans.

And he always came right in through the gate. But that day, he didn't open the gate and drive in, otherwise they might have heard him.

But anyway they weren't listening.

He must have wanted to be really quick, just pop in, take something or other and run off again. Seeing Sara in the day upset him.

He was a hypocrite that's all. He was a gentle, nice man. But he was pleased to catch her in the wrong. He was in the right, then. As well as his wife being an alcoholic, she was a depraved woman. And him so hardworking, respectable, god-fearing.

And he told Goldilox Soo she had let him down. And let Giovanni down. And let herself down. So she was given orders to get into her room, and notice to leave the house by the next morning. Even the best relationship with a boss, since Sara was her boss, or he was, is prone to termination. Cancellation.

*

So Goldilox Soo left. Expelled again. Not knowing what else to do. She and Giovanni held hands and walked away. Goldilox Soo's eyes were dry, but Giovanni cried tears for her. Sara drank a bit during the day. And Goldilox Soo didn't see her alive again. She had left her job and her house. But somehow that didn't matter. What mattered was leaving love. Or could it have been just a mirage? She saw Sara through the window. Sara put her hand up. Goldilox Soo couldn't work out whether she was waving goodbye or signalling her not to go. And for some reason she couldn't lift her hands to reply.

But the fact was she was being kicked out, again.

So she left.

And Sara cancelled herself. With all the gas from the gas cylinder she and Goldilox Soo had carried in the day before. She let it out. And struck a match. She was burnt to the size of a doll. Charred doll. In a charred doll's house.

The Grecian urn, cracked open like it had been, wasn't the least charred.

It stayed like a reminder.

But she was burnt to a cinder. She was the poor little rich girl. Cinderella. Who never turned into anything at midnight again.

Goldilox Soo's hands went numb. For days. She was scared the paralysis would come back.

But, of course, it didn't.

Giovanni said, 'Can't I play with them anymore.'

'No,' she said.

'Never?' he asked.

'Not, absolutely never. But never, for now.'

She and Giovanni were cast out but not helpless. 'Every time,' she said, with determination, 'we know just that much more, don't we Giovanni?'

'Do you think we can go back to Uncle Tizan Tronsonez?' he asked. Old enough now to think out plans.

'No.'

'What will we do?'

'Let's go to Kan Yolof, look for a room.'

'Where do all the foetuses go?' Sadna asked, almost sang. Then, in ordinary tones: 'The ones that don't come to us at the hospital for the offal van to come and fetch and do I don't know what with? The ones that don't go to Mama Naga, who does I don't know what with them either? The others, where do they go? And when? And shrouded in what secrecy?'

The smell of the chemicals from the dry-cleaning factory next to the bus stop hit them.

'All those miscarriages. Where do other women go with their foetuses, where?' asked Sadna.

'Does each woman on her own walk around with a plastic bag, drip drip drip, looking for a way to get rid of it like me? And it isn't even too hot today. That little drizzle, then the downpour, after heating the place up, have cooled it down again. No green flies walking around with me now,' Jumila whispered. 'If other women get this problem on a hot, hot day, then what?'

They all three spoke in intense, hushed tones.

Sadna went on: 'All those advice columns you read and all those advice programmes you hear never mention what to do with a foetus. How to remove ink stains. What to do if your boyfriend two-times you. How to pluck your eyebrows. How not to get wrinkles. Recipes. Depression. Headaches. Uses for an old fridge that's broken down. How to fix your iron. What to feed your husband. How to know if your son is smoking. You name it.'

'I buried one,' said Goldilox suddenly, as if she had only just remembered. 'My neighbour, Medze, and I dug it into the backyard of my brother's and my housing-estate house, and a dog dug it up. Well, not exactly, he didn't dig it up. He acted funny, and my brother suspected something and he, my own brother, a twin at that, he dug it up. He was furious. And then he, my own brother, had only one bit of advice. He kicked me out, that was his advice,' said Goldilox. 'Out. From the very house we had inherited jointly. But how was I to prove anything? We hadn't got any identity papers or anything. I was scared of him. That was the first time I was kicked out, I was on my own then. Then I went and lived in the green forest. It was so green. There were leaves every colour green.'

Sadna and Jumila were entranced. 'You lived in the forest, Goldilox Soo?' asked Jumila.

'Oh, in that forest. There was dark green bottle green pale green yellow green blue green bright green olive green fluorescent green aquamarine green turquoise green black green dull green grass green. And there was green green. There are lots of places to bury a foetus there. And it would be warm for it, and would turn into earth with the leaves, and be useful.'

'Maybe everywhere you dig you're digging where a foetus has already been buried long ago, only no one remembers,' said Jumila, looking at the tarmac of the Sité Valiji bus stop.

'Maybe right now at this very moment, at this very bus stop there is another woman carrying a foetus in a plastic bag, checking that the blood doesn't drip drip drip. Like checking your periods aren't drip drip drip. So as not to offend anyone.'

Jumila looked around her as she spoke. 'Why are we women always worrying about something so *present*. So *now*. So physical. Periods. Pregnancy. Bodies. Now. Now. Now. Tied to the present. Even when the foetus gets out, it still ties us to the present like this.'

'I think I saw one once.' It was Sadna's turn to remember. 'In the rubbish drum behind the Semino, the night my mother died. Was killed. I was getting rid of my ballet shoes, pushing them into the drum and there was, I think it was, in a plastic bag, transparent, this foetus. Had life been

114

breathed into her, I remember thinking, she may also have danced, otherwise why was she being buried in a coffin with red ballet shoes? Maybe it was the shock, made me think such thoughts.'

'You say "her", how do you know it was female?' Jumila had started wondering about this.

'I just decided. You see I had this silly thought that night, another silly thought. When I saw what I thought was a foetus, only minutes after seeing my mother dead, I thought my mother was waiting for it to get life so that she could die, and someone came in and killed her before the foetus was ready so it gave up. My mother used to think like that. I never had before. Just at that moment. And I never have since then. I don't usually think like that either.'

'Some women just cry their eyes out alone. At least there's three of us,' Jumila thanked them.

'Two women were arrested in Banbu last year because a foetus was found floating in the Belil River,' Jumila went on. 'At least there were two of them. They don't like it when it's two. That's why they arrested them. Conspiracy they say. Two charges. Illegal abortion, one. Conspiracy to commit an illegal act, two. Let alone three of us. They'll burn us at the stake. They'll think there's mutiny going on. What! In the men's backyards!'

'If it's term, even if it's stillborn, the priests agree to bury it in the cemetery,' said Sadna. 'But if it isn't term, they don't. Do they have medical checks to estimate the number of weeks, whether it's stillborn or a miscarriage?

115

The Civil Status office, too. All very approximate, if you ask me.'

'Look at the men in this bus queue. Do they have this kind of thing on their hands?' Goldilox Soo asked the rhetorical question. 'Do they have this kind of thing on their minds? Or other things we don't know they have? Hard to tell. Or are they free to think about their work, their union meetings, their plans to play dominoes under the banyan tree or pétanque near an old shop, whether Manchester United will win their match tomorrow, if Bérenger will break his alliance with Ramgoolam? It's as if they can stand there thinking about outside things instead of inside things, or as well as inside things. While we are caught in the inside things.'

'Look at the bag right now, girls. There's outside trouble for you. In the form of green flies on the bag.' Seven. Eight. Nine. Black blue green silver. The noise they were making. The beginnings of a spectacle. Buzzing. Like a helicopter finding you out, from above.

Panic struck them. They felt in the wrong. Like their left breast exposed by mistake, popped out of the bra some-how, right there in the queue to buy dhall purees in Kirpip in the winter. Like their skirt blown up by a whirlwind, exposing their bottom halves. Like their insides prolapsing out, in broad daylight, their wombs or their bowels. Like a sanitary towel, stained red and brown, somehow falling out of their panties in a bank foyer.

Then they controlled themselves.

They would have to run away.

From the flies.

'Keep cool. How many more plastic bags can a person put a foetus in?' Jumila wanted a number. A limit. A moment when you say 'no', this can't go on.

'I'll put it in the fridge at Millers'. In the messroom. I've decided.'

They kissed goodbye. Until five-thirty.

Goldilox Soo grabbed Jumila and they ran and just got on the next bus. Sadna Joyna had to go to court.

'No, I'm coming with you,' Sadna jumped in after them. 'I'll walk up to the Industrial Court from there. What if you get into trouble?' It was as though their destinies were now inextricably linked.

They all sat down near one another. 'I'd never forgive myself. Like the day I left in the middle of a demonstration, to keep a dentist's appointment or something, and then my friends got arrested. History is unforgiving sometimes.'

The green flies hadn't boarded the bus with them.

We find the two of them, Sadna Joyna and Mrs Cyril Blignault, sitting in the middle of the lounge on an old sheet on top of the carpet, playing house like they do almost every day.

It was silly. But they liked it.

'Today let's play Aladdin,' said Mrs Blignault. She had the prerogative of suggesting which game they would play. Sadna Joyna didn't have to agree, but she always did. She always wanted to play the same game that Mrs Cyril Blignault wanted to play.

Sadna Joyna worked for Mrs Cyril Blignault, whose real name was Rita and whose maiden name was Harold. Rita Harold. This maiden name, which was a first name and not a surname, meant that someone somewhere along the line, maybe her own mother, or maybe even she herself, who knows, had not had a legitimate father or any legal father at all; the law said that in such cases the mother cannot give her child her maiden name, because she was married and had therefore lost her maiden name. It was illegal to use it. Nor could she give her child her husband's name because he was not the father and wouldn't allow it. That was also illegal. Nor could the father, perhaps, declare her, because he was already duly married to someone else.

So she ended up with just two first names: Rita Harold. Now she had two other names: Mrs Cyril Blignault.

'I'll go get the things,' Sadna said.

'*Mo pase Larivyer Tanye,*' they sang in duet as they rubbed and rubbed on the brass and on the copper.

'*I pass Tanye River by, I meet an old granny there, I ask her what she's doing here, she says she's fishing for* kabo. *Dear dear dear children, all have to work to get some bread.*' The slave song you sing to babies so they learn, Mrs Blignault says.

They only played indoor games. Mrs Blignault wasn't

118

allowed out. Except to church, and then only if Sadna went with her. Or not unless he took her out. He said he gave her all she needed in her house. And he obliged by doing all the outdoor things – like shopping, and leaving the kids at school and fetching them after lessons, and gardening, all these things he did himself. She was provided for in the home, so why venture out? That's what he said. If there's anything you need, he said, you just speak up, and I'll provide it. Mrs Blignault stayed at home with her apron on, and a big trousseau of keys in the front pocket. Everything was under lock and key. He said it had to be. She was the jailer and the jailed.

Mrs Blignault's mother was allowed to visit on Friday mornings, so they didn't play house on Fridays. Sadna Joyna did the ironing, so she could hear Mrs Blignault's mother's stories of the outside world of shops and factory strikes and road accidents and first-hand stories of burglaries and hold-ups and rumours about infidelities and sexual escapades and who had had abortions and unisex hairdressing salons and the kids falling into bad ways and how they treat their parents, with examples, '*Ayoo*' in horror, and '*Get sa!*' in disbelief. The thanks you get from kids. And what with them going to discos, and pool houses, and frequenting drug dealers, and taking drugs, and of course new stories about the Naked Midnight Man. And she brought her daughter her month's supply of contraceptive pills because he didn't know about it and didn't agree anyway. And she told of communal gatherings and dark clouds.

119

Mrs Blignault's hairdresser came on Friday afternoons. Her husband said, in case they had a function at the weekend, she should look smart, meaning her hair should not be all over the place like it was right now.

'Pity my mother doesn't see me after my hair's done.'

So there they sat, rubbing the copperware and brassware with tamarind leaves and then with bought Brasso.

'He says they have to be shiny because the CP's coming round for a drink tomorrow night,' Mrs Blignault said. 'Not that they intend drinking out of brass *gilas*,' she said. 'They drink whisky. Good whisky. Bribe whisky. Out of cut-glass. They arrest people who smoke *gandya* like their own fathers did, he and the CP do. Put it in the papers. Helicopter landings. Bags of the incriminating. They drink whisky out of cut-glass. But the copperware and brassware has to be shiny.'

Sadna had soon learnt all the initials that went with her boss's husband's job. CP for Commissioner of Police and PMO and RIB for Prime Minister's Office and Rapid Intervention Brigade and, naturally, ADSU for the Anti-Drug and Smuggling Unit, not to mention endless grades like ACP and PS and DCP and the duty-free car of the exact size that goes with the specific rank of each job.

'He wants to be CP himself,' she went on.

'Don't they all,' said Sadna Joyna, rubbing until she could see a pair of perfect ballet shoes in the *catora* in her hand. She was happy when they played house together.

'Thinks he won't get promoted for communal reasons.'

'Don't they all,' said Sadna Joyna, watching her hand

dance around the *catora*. 'Communalism seems like a big hook for him to hang his failure to get promotion on. He can even say it to you and to me who never got nominated, appointed or promoted for nothing in our whole lives. I once even heard an AO, whatever that might be, complain that he hadn't got some nomination or other to an assembled crowd of mainly labourers. In a *bus queue*, it was. Everyone looked at him like he was a miracle. Reminds me. Talking of miracles, I filled in the forms for hospital servant again this year. Who knows? My mother used to think you could get me appointed.'

'They never see the funny side. He doesn't anyway. Did you hear the fight last night?' she went on.

'Yes,' said Sadna, 'but I couldn't hear what it was about.'

'He told me I was lucky he wasn't a drunk and that he didn't beat me and the kids up every night. Can't remember why. Maybe I said something like I'd like to go to the butcher's and baker's myself, making up some excuse as usual. Anyway, he took this his own way. And said I should count myself lucky. Count your lucky stars, as he put it. He reeled off this list of strokes of good luck I had had. He gave me this and gave me that, gave the kids this, gave the kids that. I went to functions other women would give their back teeth to go to. He gets doctors in to visit me at home, while other women have to queue up at the hospital. Oh! What heaven to go to the hospital! I've got this very good servant. That's you. Do I know the problem other women have with their servants? The kids have their lessons paid for. Are lacking for nothing. I'm lucky to be the mother of his children. And if he weren't called Cyril Blignault, if he weren't a Kreol, he would be CP by now. And another thing, my mother's allowed to visit. I'm not allowed to go and see her, of course. But that's because the Kreols in her area are not good enough for him. This communal stuff started to rile me. Just a little. Under the collar. Always does. Who's not good enough for who. So that's how it all started.

'Then he came up with it. And this is what drove me mad. Lucky I'm not a drunk, he says, lucky I don't come home and beat you and the kids up every night. I don't know why, but I flew into this tantrum at him. I said what kind of a life is it that a person has to be lucky not to be beaten up in her own house at night. And so on. I was screaming, I could hear myself. I wonder what got into me. It's true what he said. I'm lucky he doesn't beat me up. But at the time he said it, the order he said things in, I just thought I'd never heard anything so insulting in all my born days.'

Mother. Sadna thought of her mother's serene smile. Killed in her own house, if you could call that alley of ours our house. And Sheeba smelling of fear. She saw her ballet shoes in the rubbish drum.

'Let's go to Lemorn,' Mrs Blignault said one Tuesday morning just after they had drunk their tea.

'What? Go out?' Sadna Joyna exclaimed. 'How? Why Lemorn?'

122

'By bus. Get yourself ready. He's accompanying the PM to Rodrig and won't be back until tomorrow. The children have lessons after school. I want to paint Lemorn. My paint things are all packed already,' she said, pointing to a basket and a folded easel. 'Prepare a picnic. Didn't I tell you I wanted to go and paint something?'

'Yes, you did.' Sadna was scared. She'd got used to being locked up. She was only locked up by proxy. But Mrs Blignault hadn't got used to it. She was just biding her time.

They caught a bus to Banbu, changed to the Be di Kap bus, and got off at the Lemorn public-beach bus stop. It was a very low tide. Rita put on her hat, set up her easel and got out her paints. Then she got an artist's pad out and gave it to Sadna, with some crayons, all blacks, browns and greys. Like the Lemorn mountain.

Rita started on a romantic, scenic interpretation of Lemorn. In wild oil-paint colours. Sadna thought it was beautiful. Turquoise lagoons. Deep blue sea. Green mountain. Blue sky.

'You try, too,' Rita said to Sadna.

Sadna opened her pad, and looked up at the mountain to start drawing. It leaned over on to them. Sadna felt sudden fear.

'The mountain's going to crush us,' she said.

'Rubbish,' said Rita, not looking up. 'It's leaning the other way.'

Lemorn was a huge basalt rock on the extreme south-western corner of Mauritius. And they at its foot, looking up. It had been added on by some volcanic afterthought. New, it was. And unlikely. And menacing.

Sadna kneeled down and put her crayon to her pad. She did one sudden movement, outlining the mountain menace. Then she wanted to capture its mass.

But as Sadna looked up again, with the south-east trade winds blowing clouds fast out to sea away from them above the mountain, there was this giddy optical illusion: the mountain seemed to be bearing down on them, threatening them, imposing on them. Literally falling on to them. Pressing on their breasts.

'It's alive, Rita.'

And then something happened that upset Sadna.

'I've peed in my pants, Rita.'

But Rita wasn't upset. She just went on working and looking up at the mountain, seeing something quite different from what Sadna was seeing. She even laughed. 'Silly Sadna. What would your mother say. Never mind.' She went on painting. 'You'll have to wade into the sea then, won't you.' She laughed, painting, painting, painting her friendly mountain.

So Sadna, disturbed, took off her skirt, and waded into the sea. She felt more exposed without her skirt on. The mountain more threatening.

It was low tide, so she could walk and walk and walk in the lagoon. Perhaps the fear would lift.

In no time, she found herself in the shallows on the reef. A twenty-foot-wide wall of reef, with waterfalls everywhere, and the sounds of receding water. She didn't look up at the mountain now. She was alone, and controlling her fear of the oppressive rock.

She decided instead to go and look over the edge of the reef into the deep sea.

She had no idea what she would see. No one had ever told her what a reef was. Maybe everyone knew. Or maybe no one really understood.

And when she got to the edge, the big sea was way down below her. This shocked her. No one had ever told her the reef would look down on the sea like that.

She felt it was drawing her in. A heady fear of heights hit her so strongly that she pulled her wet pants down and shat in the nearest pool.

She washed herself and her pants and rushed back to tell Rita what had happened.

'Rita, it's going from bad to worse. Nature is dominating me.'

Rita put down her brush, and came and took her hand. She led Sadna to a spot on that sandy beach out in front of them. Between her easel and the mountain. She stopped. 'You're shaking,' she said. 'Is it the mountain coming to eat you?'

'No, the reef,' said Sadna. '*Mo finn kaka.*'

'Oh, don't be silly. Mountains and reefs haven't got time for us.

'Look at me, Sadna. Are you looking into my eyes? Stand here. Look this way. I want you to dance for me, Sadna. Just where you are now. Stand still as you can for a while, until you're calm. Back to the mountain. Back to the reef. Look into the blue sky, meditate. Stillness. Blueness. Deep peacefulness.'

As she spoke, Sadna began to be slowly hypnotized into peace.

'Now, it's time to start with your fingers and toes, move them. Feel them. Peace. Now slowly, slowly, begin gradually, begin slowly to dance with your whole body. I want you to dance against the mountain's threat. I want you to dance against the reef's threat. I want you to dance for the Queen and for Sheeba. I want you to dance for the freedom of our day here. My brush is ready. Waiting for the right moment, the right movement. Breathe slowly. Deeply. That's right. Yes, you're starting to move.'

When Sadna danced, the first dance since the murder of the Queen and Sheeba, the first dance since she stuffed her red ballet shoes into that drum, she danced with an intensity that frightened Rita, in turn.

Rita captured this wild dance of Sadna's, in her postcard painting of Lemorn. A bit of absurd, cubist, movement. Right in the middle of a picture-postcard scene.

And maybe it was this painting that made Cyril blame Sadna. His imprisoned wife had escaped. Gone out of bounds. Gone wild. He would not stand for it. Director of the Drug Squad and all.

*

When he found out, he beat Rita up. Then he tied her up. Then he hauled Sadna in and raped Sadna in front of her. Sadna was just a lesson to his wife.

The next day, when he had gone to work – Rita, face swollen from the beating, and Sadna, nursing her wounded parts – they sat in silence together. There were no words they could say. Pain. Horror. The end of a line. Even a kind of embarrassment, a kind of shame. Each one feeling to blame for the suffering of the other.

Rita said: 'I know he'll make you leave now. I have noticed you are packing your things, in case. Don't leave unless he sacks you. Then you sue him. Savage, that's what he is,' she added. 'Maybe you'll get a job at the hospital soon. Then I'll play house all alone again. Unless I do something about it.'

Then Rita got a strange expression on her face. She said that she had had this dream. Or nightmare, rather, she added. She became compelling. She caught Sadna by the arm and said: 'Listen! I must tell you. Listen to this dream. For me, I want to make this clear: *This dream is worse than what happened yesterday*. It's proof of what I have turned into. This dream came to me last night. I leave you this dream. Before we part. A legacy. Listen.'

He, that is her husband the Drug Squad man, was going past a *bannwar* tree when he looked up and saw a wasps' nest hanging as wasps' nests do by a wisp of something from a branch. I don't know where this was. Whatever he thought, Rita couldn't tell from the dream, but he suddenly climbed right up the *bannwar* tree, tied a bit of rope carefully around the wasps' nest and came down and sat on the ground with the rope in his hand, still as can be. Not moving one iota.

'It was at this point that *I* came past. Imagine me out in the open air. I stood and looked at him. There he sat with the rope in his hand, not moving.' She got quite agitated as she told about the dream.

'I said: "Hey, Cyril, what you doing with that rope in your hand, then?" I said it quite cheekily.

' "Sh! For goodness sake, don't make such a noise. Give the kids a break. Don't you know this is a *school*. You've got no respect for our institutions? I'm personally more or less in charge here, you know," he said. "I'm employed to ring the bell. At eight I ring it for the kids to go in, and then at ten I ring it again for the kids to come out again. Six thousand a month plus half a bag of rice, some dhall and some dried fish. A good position, I have here. But, unfortunately, I shall have to resign soon. Doctor's orders. I must go to the countryside, preferably the seaside. Need a change of climate." Imagine him resigning.

' "Well," I replied in the dream. "Since you have to go, why don't you give me your job when you resign? Your *position*?"

128

' "In fact, I'm leaving today. Soon as I get a replacement," he said, elusively.

' "Well, here I am," I persisted, trying to get confidence in myself. *Me, me, me!* I cried in the dream. So silent I have been in life.

' "You! What if you miss the hour, forget to ring the bell or something. Why, you can't be trusted." He was smug.

' "Don't worry, Cyril, I'll never be one to get reproached for not doing work properly. Hand over the rope."

'He gave me the rope, grandly, saying: "Now listen to me. At ten the church bells will ring. You must ring this at the same time. Take note." He said this like the director of the Drug Squad to the assistant director. In my dream I was proud of this recognition. Imagine it.

'He went off. I sat under the *bannwar*, rope in hand, listening for the life of me. As soon as I heard the church bells ring, I pulled on my rope. Nothing happened. No bells rang. I felt failure creeping up on me.

' "It's a heavy one, this bell is, Rita! You have to pull hard!" I mumbled to myself.

'I then literally hung from the rope, pulling and pulling and shaking it. All of a sudden the branch broke, the wasps' nest fell out of the tree. The wasps were all wild, tore out of the wasps' nest, came straight for me, stung me in the face, stung me on my hands, on my feet, on my eyelids, all over. I suppose it's my bruised face that made me put that bit in.

' "Help! Save me, Mother!" Always call for my mother,

129

still, big as I am. Anyway, I ran off, wasps trailing behind me, stinging me like mad.'

'Is that the end of the dream?'

'Ah,' she said, ignoring Sadna Joyna, 'a dream of punishment it was. For trying to get in on the school act. Schools are not for the likes of us. Punishment for trying to be like him? Punishment for trying to be part of the same person. I even share his name, you know. His French name, don't know where he got it from in the first place. Now I want to share his job. His power.' They were wont to speak in this irreverent manner when they played house. But only when they played house.

'No. It goes on. I'm remembering the next bit.'

'I was recovered from the stings. I was going past a row of ornamental palms, you know those ones like in *Place d'Armes* in front of Government House. Who should I see going past, but Cyril. It was as though I hadn't seen him since the wasps' nest business. So I was cross. There was anger inside me, lying in wait for him. That's true. "Where are you going, sonofabitch. I'll kill you." Imagine if I said that to him in real life?

' "Sh!" he said to me. Always saying "sh".

' "Sh! Don't you know this is a church? For Christ's sake. You mad? Screaming out aloud like that. Can't you see the columns lining the church veranda? Fool!" He pointed at the ornamental palms.

'I believed him. In the dream I believed him. I thought I had been wrong about them being palms. I could have kicked myself for being so ignorant. And for him finding out about my ignorance.

'"I'm the verger, and I'm afraid I'll have no alternative but to kick you out if you don't behave. Off the premises."

'I was flabbergasted. Another important job, he's got.

'Cyril walked this way and that, pretentiously on the church veranda, then turned to me.

'"Why, my dear, do come and taste this holy water," he said, putting out his index finger. "I shouldn't let you taste this. You haven't got enough respect for the church." In fact, while he was walking this way and that on the church veranda, he had stuck his finger in a saucer of honey he had already hidden under a fern at the root of one of the ornamental palms. But I didn't know that at first. There was this feeling of being thwarted.

'Like the fool I am, I went and tasted the holy water.

'"Mmm. That's divine." I felt shame at liking it, but couldn't help liking it. "Divine holy water. Where do they keep this holy water in the church, then, Cyril?"

'Cyril took me by the hand, as if I were his child, and walked me over to it. "There!" He pointed.

'It looked like holy water in a bowl. In fact it was a big honeycomb. Of course, I didn't realize that, nor did I realize that there were bees still in it.

'Off he went. In rather a hurry, I noticed.

'I went up to the honeycomb, saying: "I think I'll say a

131

little prayer. For that, perhaps I'll need the tiniest bit of holy water." In the dream I was so *opportunist*. Such a leech. Like I am in real life.

'I put my hand into the honeycomb. Bees started to pour out like smoke from a fire, and attack me by the wave, sticking to me, stinging away. I went mad with the pain, rolling in agony on the ground, until I lay there, left for dead. The bees actually left me for dead.

'Sleep. The beating up again coming into the dream. And also last night there were mosquitoes biting me. They attack open wounds, you know. Probably all the mosquitoes made me dream that bit.'

'Is that the end, Rita?' Sadna asked, 'Punishment for getting too close to the church? Not a woman's place. Punishment for wanting to taste the sweet things of life?'

It was the first reference to what had happened. Punishment for sweet escape.

'It isn't finished yet. Hold on, I'm remembering now. Some time passed, and I'd got better after the stings again. Then Cyril decided to visit the CP's wife. Yes. There she was in the dream, stroking his police medals in front of me like that. It was very real.

'Anyway.

'As they were chatting, she said to him: "Do you know someone called Rita Harold, by any chance?"

'I overheard this.

' "You ask me if I know Rita Harold. Why naturally. She's my horse! My mare. In fact, at four this afternoon, if you stand at your window, you'll see me passing by on her back."

'I was furious. You liar, I thought. You haven't got a horse. You brute. I'm not your mare.

'Off went Cyril. He went into the woods. Only afterwards did it become clear to me what he had done. He knew where there was a mother hen sitting on eggs. He went and took three rotten eggs, they smell a bit from the outside if they're rotten you know, so he checked and put them in his pocket. He is so clever.

'Then he sat on a rock, waiting.

'Naturally, I went past and saw him.

'I was still furious. From the wasps. From the bees. From his remark.

' "You pig! Today I'm gonna get you. I'll kill you this time." Imagine me speaking to him like that. Threatening him.

'Then what happened?'

'Cyril started to cry. Yes, burst into tears. "Oh! What pain I'm in. My dear friend, Rita, my beloved wife, Rita. It's no use. You won't have to go to the trouble of killing me. I'm gravely, desperately, mortally ill. I'll die in any case any minute now. Oh! Ouch! What agony, what pain, what infernal suffering! I beg you, Rita, forgive me for everything. Give me a hand, so that I can get up. I want to drag myself to the hospital, see if there's any doctor who can calm my pain. Ouch! My stomach is burning. O Hideous pain!"

'As I got nearer to him, I smelt this awful smell. Foul smell. Worse than rotten eggs, I thought. In the dream.

' "Cyril, how come you smell so awful. I can't bear it."

133

' "O! O! That is my body. I'm dying. I've already started rotting. Rot set in prior to death. I can't walk at all. Please, I beg of you, carry me to the hospital, my dear wife. God will bless you for it!"

'I, good Samaritan as ever, agree. Typical.

' "Of course, of course. Get on up."

'I put him on my back.

' "Give me a bridle, my dear wife, in case I fall off."

'I comply. I give him a bridle. Typical.

' "Give me a whip, my dear wife, so that I can use its handle to show you the way. Just for that reason, my dear Rita. The road to the hospital is very hard to find, you know. I'm the only one who knows it. O, even to speak is too painful for my throat. Don't make me have to speak to explain things, it hurts too much. Give me a whip. Ouch!"

'And so I gave him a whip.

'When Cyril was on my back, with the bridle fixed to my mouth and the whip in his hand, he drove me straight towards the CP's wife's house.

'I walked and walked. Slowly, like I do. Like a mule. Or one of those cows that has been kept in a small thatch hut and walks for the first time, wobbly as a child, when it's on its way to the butcher's just before dying of old age.

'He started yelling at me. "Hurry, don't you know the hospital gates close at four. Speed up, gallop, silly mare, or the gate will be closed by the time we get there."

'I walked on and on.

'Cyril pulled at the bridle and warned: "Run, I tell you,

run when I tell you to. Orders are orders. To be obeyed."

'I was furious.

' "If you don't sit still, I'll buck you right off my back in a minute."

'Cyril just laughed. "Go ahead and try, my dear, do try."

'And with that, he started to whip me to prove his point.

'I wanted to throw him off my back, but I couldn't; the bridle cut into my mouth and the whip cut into my shoulders. So I had to keep running, with him on my back. It must be my injuries made me dream that. The cut on my lip. The bruised shoulder.

'We went past, right under the CP's wife's window. Cyril doffed his hat by way of greeting her.

'The sea wasn't far. Cyril then started driving me right into the water. I can't swim, as you know, so I wanted to stop. But he wouldn't let me. He drove me, drove me, drove me. It was like a rape. Like what he did to you yesterday. Water rose up higher and higher, until it was over my head. My arms flayed about, my hair spread around me on the water's surface, I opened my mouth to cry for help, but I couldn't. All that happened was that water flowed in, and I felt I was drowning, drowning.

'I woke up in a panic.

'And then as I dozed off, the dream took up again. Ever had a dream that continues after you're dead?'

'Yes, I've also had one like that,' said Sadna.

'Anyway, Cyril took his clothes off and put them out to dry. I was dead by then.

135

'He put them on again, and went to see the CP's wife, and said, "Rita Harold was a stupid old mule. I've sold her, along with a rather fine octopus I speared in the lagoon today." Like he speared you.'

Sadna doesn't know if the dream caused Rita's suicide, or if her life caused the dream and the suicide. Or if she was just tired of playing house.

But, that very evening, after Sadna'd gone for her bath and before Cyril Blignault got back from work or whatever, she went off all on her own. Her clothes were found in a neat pile on the beach at Be di Tombo the next morning by a police search party.

She didn't leave a message. But the story she told Sadna probably counts as one.

And then Cyril just sacked Sadna.

Put her out on the streets. Told her to get the hell out of the place. And so it was that she started drifting inexorably towards Kan Yolof.

When she found she was pregnant, she decided to keep it. She thought it was only one. But not being able to bear remembering how she had become pregnant, she attributed it to an asexual form of insemination.

'Lemorn Mountain and the Reef impregnated me,' she said. Later she would find out she was expecting twins, so the metaphor of the double father held in her mind.

136

She had been born, herself, of a rape. The Queen had told her. As if the man were insignificant.

'I wanted a child right then. You were a wanted baby girl, Sadna. And I've always wanted you. If I hadn't, I knew what to do. And you would have been born someone else.' For her reincarnation was as natural as the rain.

Sadna had an idea. She told them about it in the bus. She had turned all calm and rational.

'I think we are making a mountain out of a molehill,' she said quietly.

'And Jumila is getting tired now,' she added. 'We have to look after her. She's not well. We can't be just seeing to the foetus.'

True enough.

'Your legs must be feeling weak. And we've got other things to do now. More important things. There's civil war in the air, and what are we doing to prevent it? Wandering around with a foetus in a plastic bag. For god's sake. We've got this meeting, don't we? A party meeting? I've got this court case I'm party to. I intend getting there. I've got to win something out of that job. Others, after me, have got to get something out of that job of mine as well. We've got the dancing party afterwards. Nani expects us to come. I've got to transfer the twins from place to place. There's Giovanni. There's The Boy Who Won't Speak. You've both

137

got jobs to get back to before this afternoon is over. We've got livings to earn.'

She was talking sense. Slowly, but surely, making headway with sense. In the bus.

They were nearly ready now. To get rid of it.

'There's providence in the fall of a sparrow,' she added.

'What you talking about now, Sadna?' said Jumila.

'Do you agree that it's *time*? Time we got rid of it. A time and a place for everything. Now's the time.'

'Yes,' said Jumila.

'Yes,' said Goldilox Soo.

'Well, I'll just shove it in the nearest big rubbish bin I see when we get off at Victoria bus station. Better still, I know a drum very near Victoria Station, in an alleyway, an alleyway I know like the back of my hand, and I'll just shove it in that drum. Then we can drink a glass of *aluda* at the bazaar, then carry on with our normal lives. Look forward to the rest of the day, the rest of the week, the rest of the month, the rest of the year, and plan the rest of our lives in this country, not to mention on this planet.'

'Oh, Sadna, your *timing* is magnificent. No wonder you used to be a dancer.' Goldilox Soo was exalted.

'I'm ready now,' said Jumila.

Jumila was ready.

'Get rid of it, Sadna.'

Yes, they could part with it now.

'Wait here,' Sadna said to them.

138

They knew it was a private matter.

She went past the Semino, and she started to push open the door into their old alleyway. The Queen and Sheeba and hers. She had never been back there. 'Odd,' she thought, 'I've seen a foetus in that drum, just there, before. Must be why I thought of the place.'

She pushed the door slowly, and as it opened into the alleyway, she realized that it wasn't their home anymore. Realized it for the first time. She had lived with this illusion. Of course. 'It's time for getting rid of illusions as well as of the foetus,' she thought.

'Of course,' she whispered. 'Of course.'

Everything changes. Of course. Only, she had somehow just gone and left this alleyway suspended.

She thought the dread was left over from the past. From the memory of the process of reconstructing the crime with the policemen. And from before that, from finding the bodies. Sheeba's smell of fear. Her mother's calm expression in death. Long live the Queen. Sheeba no more pups to suckle from her seven pairs of tits. 'Mother Mary look after me. I still have my past to go through.'

The past made her feel dizzy as she went into the alley.

But no. It was more than that.

It wasn't just the past that was impinging on normality. It was the present.

Right there in front of her.

She saw a policeman in uniform, sitting on the ground,

139

legs apart, leaning against the drum, hands shaking almost uncontrollably, pain drawn on to his every feature and every sinew, shooting something into the big vein in his neck with a syringe.

'Poor sod,' she mumbled.

'Put it in the fridge, as planned,' was all she could say to the other two.

'You seen a ghost?' asked Goldilox Soo.

'Some men are bound to the present like that. Like we are. It's a drug. Or chains. Or poverty. In our case, all three.' Sadna shuddered.

'What you on about?' Goldilox Soo was worried.

'Put it in the fridge, as planned. I'm going straight to the Industrial Court. Forget the *aluda*. I'll tell you about what I saw in our alleyway another day. Enough for one day. Suffice it for me to say, Gold and Jumila, decisions are partly ours to make, partly made for us. You can't always choose time. It sometimes chooses you.'

The other two shook their heads in disbelief. Perhaps, they thought, she's going loony.

And so all three were cast up like flotsam in Kan Yolof. After squalls and storms. And tempests and shipwrecks that no one in the world was interested in. And cyclones.

Yes, cyclones invariably left flotsam. Here and there. But mainly in Kan Yolof.

'What?' said Sadna Joyna. 'You also lost your boss, Goldilox Soo?'

Goldilox Soo was last to speak. She could only manage a few words: 'I also lost my boss. Gas explosion. She'd just fetched the yellow gas cylinder that very day.'

She stopped talking suddenly.

Couldn't think about it yet, let alone talk.

'That means,' Sadna Joyna went on, 'that all three of us lost our bosses? There are so many *stories* in people. Like dances.'

They were sitting in a row one behind the other in lazy hypnotic ritual. Each sitting on a *pirha* stool, legs wide apart, skirts stuffed downwards, picking at one another's heads and hair under a *lakoklis* tree in the Kan Yolof court-yard they had ended up like flotsam in.

Jumila in front, then Goldilox Soo, then Sadna Joyna at the back.

'You've got lots of louse eggs,' she said to Goldilox, 'but I'm getting them. One by one.'

Then Sadna felt a dampness on Goldilox Soo's cheeks, a dampness on her own wrists. She turned her wrists to look. Yes. Tears. She took her *horni* and wiped Goldilox's cheeks from behind, saying nothing. Then she passed her hands slowly over Goldilox Soo's closed eyes, again and again, light as a feather, hypnotic. Goldilox Soo was quiet. Her tears rolled down in silence.

'Two weeks in Kan Yolof and we're full of them,' Jumila chatted on, sitting in front, not knowing. 'Lice, I mean, not stories.'

Goldilox Soo went on scratching Jumila's head gently. So that she wouldn't know she was crying. She crushed another nit between the nails of her left and right thumbs and went on scratching around, picking around, parting the hair strand by strand on Jumila's bent head. She, Goldilox Soo, held her own head tilted a little bit back while Sadna stopped looking for lice in her hair. 'You haven't got too many left now,' she said. Not that it was true. Goldilox Soo appreciated the soothing statement anyway. Sadna stroked her hair, and then started to comb it.

Lost their bosses. Ever heard such a thing? They all three lost their bosses. Other people call it losing your job. They called it *losing our bosses*. And they were out looking for new bosses. In fact, that's how they got to be friends and neighbours. They were all three out looking for a new boss and they got sidetracked.

As well as losing their bosses, when they lost them, they lost their houses as well. At the same time. Tied housing. Your house is tied to your boss. You lose your boss, you lose your house. 'And sometimes there's nothing you can do to hold on to a boss,' Sadna announced, 'try as you will. So there goes your rice. There goes Giovanni's salt fish. You start watching the trees for mangoes. Green mangoes. With salt from the sea. Boiling green bananas. So there goes your house. Nowhere to live.'

This is the sidetracking starting.

Jumila remembered one of Rahim's leaflets: *'Nothing worse for wage slave than to lose her boss. Nothing worse for wage slave than to lose her house. When she loses both, it's worse still. It's bad.'* The leaflet didn't say exactly that, but that's how she remembered it now. She had a way of updating memories like this. But she didn't say it aloud.

The sidetracking started when each of them was looking for a new boss, and bosses were turning their noses up at them because they didn't even have a house, and bosses were looking at the respective kids as though they could be *wished away* prior to consideration for remunerative employment. When they looked at The Boy Who Won't Speak with some alarm and at Giovanni with dread and at Goldilox Soo, herself, with fear, and at Sadna's expanding tummy and then, after their birth, at the twins, with positive horror: What! Two of them. As if Sadna were an extravagant spendthrift of some kind.

Another thing. They didn't have references either. How to get a reference from a lost boss?

Prospective new bosses didn't realize that Goldilox Soo didn't even have a birth certificate. If they had realized this, they would have fainted. *Quel horreur.*

First there was Sadna Joyna, kicked out and pregnant, washed up to have her twins in Kan Yolof. Then eight months later Goldilox Soo, who was put down there the morning of the day when the twins decided to come out. Then two months after that, Jumila. Blown in on her light

143

foot. Her limp heavy as lead. Light as a feather. Heavy as lead. Light as a feather. Heavy as lead.

So the three of them had found out separately but in the same year that you got to have a house *first*.

They have a common tune: When we say house, we mean room. When we say house, we mean lodging. When we say house, we mean housing. Anything. Any place. To hide from the heat of the sun and the wet of the rain.

First a house. Then a job. Create the earth first, then work it.

That's how come we came to be living in Kan Yolof. That's how come we got sidetracked from looking for a job. When you lose your boss and your house, there's no relative, no friend, no do-gooder, no charity, no no one good enough to help you. You are beyond help. You are bad news. Sometimes they call you a hopeless case. They just look at you and then at the kid or the kids and then back at you and they shake their heads and say to one another 'She's a hopeless case'. You're so hopeless, they can just say it right there in front of you. As if you're not there. Invisible.

That's their song.

Then you have to go to Kan Yolof. There, there's the poor. They don't think you're helpless. They help you. They don't think you're hopeless. Even they have got hope.

Those who have not.

They are the ones who give.

Those who are abandoned.

They are the ones who take you in.

Those who live in overcrowding.

They are the ones who have a chicken coop to offer you.

In Kan Yolof, they live in enclosed spaces between things.

Places where the land developers haven't got to yet. Somewhere near the docklands, near the city centre, near the drug and prostitution rings, near the motorway. Where old warehouses, and mansions, and stone stables, and new skyscrapers all mingle, and in-between there are still spaces.

Interstices.

And in these spaces, you can do your own architecture. It's one of the few places where you can still do your own architecture on this planet. Most people can only just do some of their own interior decoration. Even bosses don't do their own architecture. Talk about helpless. They're the hopeless cases.

As you can see, from such words, they're fighting back now. Because I only write what's in their heads. Their song.

In these spaces in Kan Yolof, you can do not just your own architecture, but your own quantity surveying, too.

In strange shapes, long oblong gaps, triangular spaces, tall thin holes, and often a wide clearing around a single tap. With corrugated-iron scraps, with newspapers painted with left-over varnish, with drums that the roller's been sent over and flattened, bits of hardboard of strange shapes, plywood torn off packing-crates, sheets of plastic that may have been someone's shower curtains, cardboard from boxes, chicken-wire, sheets of styrofoam, opened out gunny bags and fertilizer sacks, and other things you might find here and there if you know where to look, too.

They soon found out about where to look. Once they were there, they found out where to look for everything. For things they didn't dream existed.

And they started to hear about the *house movement*, house *movement*, *house* movement. All manner of things that had been happening before they met each other. What could it be? House Movement? And other magical words like the Union? And of all unbelievable things a Women's Movement? Who ever thought women would or could or did *move*?

And the political party now. What does it mean? Who would want them in one anyway? Ah, they would find out.

And not being the guilty party. Yes, they thought they were always the guilty party. But no. A court case might recognize them as a party. And maybe not the guilty.

And even a wild party.

Yes, they would learn about parties.

That's the best. Frozen. Freeze your problems. Freeze them temporarily. Secretly. And get on with it. Get on with every-thing else. Isn't this *the most* we ever do? Most of the time. Put our problems on to the refrigeration setting. See about them later. Well, it wasn't for lack of trying.

So Sadna went to her court case. The one o'clock sitting.

That would start at half-past one. 'Sue the bastard,' as she put it, and then: 'Sue him in any case. Even if he isn't a bastard. Even if he's been perfectly nice.' That's what the Union said. With bosses, the Union said, you have to get them where they show a weak flank. That's where. Complain to the Protector of Workers.

Jumila handed the plastic bag over to Goldilox Soo. Their hands touched. She felt a sense of loss, impending loss. Like pain. Like anger. A tugging tie with the life that never was. And then she let go of it. It receded. The plastic bag. And the loss.

She smiled at Goldilox Soo.

She would go and see if The Boy Who Won't Speak was managing with the bras.

Separated from it now, she was.

'Thank you, Gold,' she said. And off went Goldilox Soo towards her building. With the plastic bag now hers.

Jumila watched her going.

Jumila moved on. She walked, one foot heavy, one foot light, one foot heavier now, one foot lighter now, on her way to the Outer Islands Development Corporation godown.

She saw The Boy Who Won't Speak and felt a warmth in her. A letting go. A relaxedness. A caring. If she'd been a dog, she would have licked him.

She sat on the crate next to The Boy Who Won't Speak, their feet on the grass mat, and held his hand, and said, 'Sorry I was away so long. You know,' she said, in a warm apologizing way, 'it was *only women's business*.' She could

147

say this kind of thing to The Boy Who Won't Speak because he can't speak. Or he won't anyway. Then she said, to show that everything was fine and life going on as usual, 'Show me the money.' He had sold three bras. 'You're so clever. You're perfect.'

He smiled. His wan smile. Pleased.

A wholeness came over her. Yes, she would manage now. Her legs felt weak. Specially the one. But everything will be all right.

'I'm here now. I'm with you now. I'm waiting for Goldilox Soo to come back. Then you can go on home and do some sewing before it gets dark. We're going to the meeting. Rahim said he'll come and sit with you for a while, when you're sewing. Then in no time I'll be home. Then there's the dancing party, remember. Meanwhile, here's money, go buy me a Coke. I'm so thirsty. Buy yourself some *gato pima* as well.'

Two women from the countryside came up to her and asked directions to the Victoria bus station. 'They must be from the north,' she thought. She spent a lot of her time directing country people from one place to another in Porlwi. All street merchants do, she thought to herself. It's a social service we perform. She performed hers with love.

There was this feeling in the air. Men were getting jumpy. Especially the men of power. Especially the men of money.

148

It was in all the papers at the time. You opened them at breakfast, put on your glasses to make sure. Old men took out their magnifying glasses, crossed their knees, and settled down to check. Yes, there it was. Splashed. All three of them being well-known women. Well, not exactly well-known women. Wives of well-known men to be precise. Men that had a *the* not an *a* in front of them. *The* head of the Drug Squad. *The* managing director of the Millers' Group of Companies. *The* famous historian. The the the. In the space of less than nine months.

In those circles, men started to suspect it might just be an epidemic. Suspect. And to look at their own wives in a funny way just in case they also upped and did it. Suspect. Suspect that women did it for spite. Especially when you saw the way their surviving husbands were left zombies. All three of them. Walking around with their arms not swinging anymore. All three of them walking up to closed doors or to closed gates, opening them, going through them, and then passing through, going on, leaving the doors and the gates yawning open behind them. Just walking on with their arms not swinging anymore.

To make it worse, they had been very different. The men that is. Although they all acted the same now. They had nothing in common that you could blame, and say well, *I'm* not like that. They were men that conjured up adjectives. Different adjectives. The Drug Squad chief a weak, sadistic, necrophilic man, domineering and obsequious and stupid. The managing director of Millers'

149

Group of Companies a shy and gentle person, kind and considerate, thoughtful and quiet, a nice man, wouldn't hurt a fly. The historian a harmless pompous ass, pretentious but ineffectual, sometimes obsequious, other times condescending, invariably speaking French to impress, not a man to be taken seriously, what with his copy of *Twelfth Night* open on his desk as if he were reading the bloody thing.

Come to think of it the women were different too. Well at that time anyway. All the time before the hour. They only came to have this haunting resemblance to one another in their deaths. The hour of their deaths. In the hour of their suicides. They seemed identical. All the rest of the time, they had been as different from one another as chalk and cheese.

A shudder got into the social tissue of the rich and middle classes. The higher the worse.

One man, a major shareholder in god knows what, opened his wife's car door, when she was sitting at the wheel, car stationary in the driveway of their seaside house in Granbe, sitting there she was, in the driver's seat on a Sunday afternoon, waiting for the kids to pile in – it was Mothers' Day – and he clouted her hard enough to split her lip. A string of red pearls.

Then he closed the car door.

Sometimes men were more scared because they felt it as a

form of murder. Murder of husbands. And would they be next? It could happen to me too.

Twelve men killed their wives in three months. Pre-emptive strikes. Got to teach them a lesson, other men whispered.

Collective memory lives on. The Dutch left forever because of rats and women.

First there was rats. An epidemic of rats. People still fear them. Like male organs that have escaped from the body and soul. To haunt everyone. Slipped out from under the belt. May strike below the belt. The rats are under control now. Only just. But the fear lives on.

And then there was the other epidemic. The worrisome one. Women had started to murder their husbands. One after the other. It was infectious, the Dutch East India Company reported to the authorities in the Cape. This can't go on. Something will have to be done about it. A stop will have to be put to all this murder. And it was not murder in any old way. It was murder by poisoning. The worst way, as far as the men could see. Just at the point of weakness, the point where they accept the very food they need to live on. And who knows, the slaves might do it next.

What if another epidemic was starting now? Some kind of four-hundred-year cycle? Rats? Or the wives of the ruling classes rising up, or rather sneaking up one by one, and murdering their husbands, murdering by *suicide* this time.

Was it not already an epidemic? Not just the three of

them. What are women up to? What are they thinking about? What is in their heads? Why do they get the giggles from time to time like that? As though they've lost control? What do they say to one another when they wash clothes together or prepare wedding meals together? Witches!

One look at the newspapers. Death by suicide. Suicide on the increase. And yet no one ever asked *why* did the women do it? This was what caused the stir. The silence. No one asked: Did they all get the same idea at more or less the same time? Like it was coming in from abroad. From the outside. Like a change in the weather. A source of suicide. Nor did anyone pose questions as to whether it was one long chain reaction. The first one having some outside cause, and then they all started to catch it from one another in quick succession? Yes, that's a point. Was it catchy? Infectious like measles or mumps? Passing from one woman to another by some form of contact. People were scared to find out. They didn't ask.

By steel, by water, by jumping into the abyss, they did it. But mainly by fire. Like The Boy Who Won't Speak's mother. She just took the kerosene bottle, and right there in front of that child, she sprinkled herself with it, and a neighbour heard her say, 'Step back a little, Boy,' in her nicest voice, and she just struck a match.

She just burnt to death there and then. In front of him. Like a taper.

And now the one who taught him to sew, the historian's wife, had also done it.

But Liz didn't do it by fire. Steel blades, she used. Used against herself. Got rid of herself. For her own treachery. For teaching her little ones by default to be her enemies. For perpetuating what ought not to have been perpetuated.

Sara did it by fire, by explosion. She let all the gas out of the yellow cylinder and then struck a match. Burnt to a Cinderella doll. In a charred doll's house. Got rid of herself and her house. The Grecian urn cracked open.

Rita by water. Because of a dream, because she suddenly understood what it means to accept slavery and imprisonment, maybe. Got rid of herself instead of attacking the slavery or the jail.

And the husbands turned into zombies.

Goldilox Soo went through the magic door, became invisible and went right through the 'Mauritian Miracle' television sets and the CNN scenes of civil war and straight to her mop and her mop pail between the service lift and the stairwell and picked them up and went right into the service lift which was already open and pressed the button for the sixth floor which was where the workers' mess was, and the fridge.

Now Goldilox Soo was not allowed to use the workers' mess because she wasn't a Millers' Group of Companies worker but just a Klinnkwik piece-rate girl. Millers' wasn't her boss so they didn't give her a messroom. They weren't even paying the compulsory pension money, so why would they give her a messroom.

But Goldilox Soo was stealthy enough. And in any case, she was in charge of *cleaning* the messroom floor once a week. It wasn't cleaning-the-messroom-floor day but who would know. So she went up to the door with her mop in one hand and her mop pail and the plastic bag in the other.

So she checked there was no one there, and went in. She prayed to Mary, briefly, woman to woman, specially being a woman helping a woman in distress. An image of Kali went through her mind. For later. And she saw severed heads strung around her own neck like pearls. Like Kali's.

Then she opened the fridge door and looked into the fridge. There was plenty of space as usual. Just a few of those squares of UHT milk and a packet of biscuits that had been there for a long time. No one left anything in the fridge because they said it always got stolen. These biscuits must have been soggy or something, if that was the case.

Beat that. Stealing from your own mess. Slaves, we are. Aren't we? The cold air crept out and fell on to her feet. Like ghosts. She shuddered and closed the door quickly.

She took a pencil out of her apron pocket and looked in the dustbin for a bit of paper. She found a long band of paper, perhaps a supermarket receipt, and wrote on it *This parcel belongs to Goldilox Soo. Do not touch*. Serve them bloody well right if they steal it, she thought. She folded the plastic bag around itself, wrapped the paper around the whole thing, and tied the paper on with a bit of string that had been tied on to the handle of the Air Islands Duty Free bag.

Now a decision to take. Freezer or fridge?

Fridge will do. She put it in the fridge. Then no. 'Freeze the problem.' Freezer better. More room for contingencies. And so it was that on second thoughts, she put it right into the freezer section, with the message pointing outwards, right in the very front of the freezer.

'No use trying to hide it,' she said aloud.

A risk putting her name on it like that. But a calculated one. The person who opened it would be in the wrong. Do not touch the private property of someone else. In this case, do not touch the private property of Goldilox Soo. The person who said anything, would seem to be the one who stole all the things that went missing out of the fridge. So they probably wouldn't say anything.

She would get ticked off for using the Millers' workers' fridge in the Millers' workers' mess. But that didn't matter. She would say she wouldn't do it again.

They would come back and get it *after* the meeting. This way they wouldn't have to take it with them to the meeting. You wouldn't feel right having it with you in the company of men. It would put them out if they knew.

Then afterwards, the three of them could come and get it, take it to the women's party and then, on the way home,

155

do a detour past the hospital so that Sadna could meet the offal man. Last ditch stand.

She closed the freezer, and the fridge door.

Amen.

When they first came to Kan Yolof, one by one, they settled in. Like it was a nest. They soon got to picking nits out of one another's hair. And they got to thinking. To thinking about things. They got to thinking separately, one behind the other and in parallel, and to thinking with their heads together, as well.

They learnt to concentrate. Their attention and their actions.

For example today. Today is a certain *today* about seven or eight months ago. Today their friendship gets consecrated.

There is already excitement in the air when Kumar from the House Movement arrives at their courtyard. Even this early. Hours before the bus is due. He knows Rahim. Rahim is getting people together at another place. Some place they've never heard of. At the same time.

> . . . *send the word to all the people in the land,*
>   *To every hill and mountain for the time is now at hand,*
>   *Light a fire*

Time.

On this day, time is suspended. It is as though time has got a different feeling to it. You know how every day there is the usual feeling of everything running down, ebbing away, running out. Time just seeping out, oozing away.

Well today it's different.

There's a beginning, and then there'll be a huge swelling middle in which anything could happen and out of which anything could be born, and maybe even a promising ending, happy and hopeful. Who knows?

In the beginning, Kumar just sits on the log under the red pepper tree, playing with Sadna Joyna's baby twins in turn, while everyone feels the pace quickening and the effervescence of the day building up. Like before a concert. Each musician warming up. Preparing for concerted action.

'Nearly ready,' says Jumila and goes to ready some others.

> *Watch and wait*
> *Get ready for the signs*
> *There are many here among us now*
> *Who have not seen the light*

Kumar's presence is providential. A proof that the day has come. That the hour has come. And that the minute and the second will come soon. A reminder that all is on schedule. That today is different. That something will happen. That the bus, for a start, will arrive at midday. That time will intensify, take on meaning. That all the old, heavy memories will lift off, up into the stratosphere.

Kumar looks up and sees a sparrow. And shows it to the twins.

'Are you taking an umbrella?'

'Lend me five rupees!'

'Kalil hasn't got back from night shift yet.'

Like birdsong.

If you were going past in the street outside, you would never believe that this place existed. Hidden inside the city. But you would feel the tension in the air today. You would stop, and put your head back and sniff. You would feel called.

But you would see just this one tin gate between two high walls. Unpromising.

But. But, if you were to just push it, push on this tin gate. Go on.

It creaks open, and you see a short passageway, cobbled. Go in, the door closes behind you, by its own creaking weight. You go along the passageway, which opens out into a clearing, a courtyard. Spacious, with the red pepper tree huddled in the middle of it, and the log hiding under the red pepper tree, a log that always has two or three people sitting on it, and a lop-sided old deck-chair facing the log. The deck-chair always has a granny in it. Maybe sorting rice like today. Old men, lazy children, loud women sorting lentils, gathered under the red pepper tree. Four or five chickens eating the discarded bits of rice and lentils. A dog

158

wagging its tail. Because today they're readying themselves.

Twenty-three adults and twenty-eight children quiver with retained excitement in these rooms invented and created all around the edges of this courtyard. One tap in the middle. Space within a space. Like the time that is being born within time. Bursting with energy.

And, like migrating birds, they begin to gather. Time for change. Time is filling out now with shared meaning. Slowly but loudly, they gather. Talking, laughing, squabbling. Gathering all the while, but instead of in the banyan tree waiting to migrate, under the red pepper tree. Mainly women and children. All getting excited. Action ahead. Expectancy. The menfolk calm, proud. Inertia and impotence fade away into this expanding bit of day.

The inhabitants of the temporary shelters in Ter Ruz are now, right now, gathering in the same way in front of their row of tin houses in the mud. The young man from the House Movement, Kumar, says so. This knowledge adds new time and new space to the moment.

Day in day out, time had dragged on, relentless, *outside of them*. But now time seems harnessable. Brought in. So that it can be explored, opened out, exploded even. There is a charge in the air. Transformation. Seeds stirring with life.

They know they will meet the others from everywhere else, from god knows where else, at Senn Mars at one o'clock. Then what will happen? What will happen next?

159

In the meantime, it's best slacks, best *churidars*, best saris, best dresses, and the kids dressed to kill. The Boy Who Won't Speak has Giovanni's other smart trousers on and Sadna Joyna comes out and dusts white powder on the twins' cheeks. Kumar offers his cheeks playfully. Sadna Joyna is all tinsel in what must have been someone's old red and gold wedding sari and matching *champal*. Her *tica* shines.

Goldilox Soo is dressed like an American model on the television. She's got these sunglasses that have a mirror on the outside that she found at the public lavatories when she was working there. She's got polish on her toenails. Her hair gives out its usual glow. A firefly.

Even Jumila's usually dull youthful-youthless cheeks burn with enthusiasm and confidence. In her riotously coloured *churidar*.

The colours themselves challenge the idea of time. They defy the very notion of fading. We will never be raw cloth again. Never be sackcloth. Never be a gunny bag.

The children are all expectancy. Like when a surprise is near. When they don't quite know the meaning of the word *surprise*. They run around, trailing the banners and hoisting the posters, voices starting to turn into songs. Whispers into words: *demonstration*. Like a charm? What will this be? What does it mean? What can it mean? And to be in it? What will we do in one?

Maybe just inform the king? Or rather the Minister of Housing.

Or just be in it. Part of it. Part of something.

160

There had been preliminary meetings. Phrases from them suspended in today's electric air. *Make private suffering public knowledge. In slavetimes they gave us a hut. In indenture they had houses built for every person, man or woman. What kind of a place is this anyway?*

What are we asking for?

A house!

What are we gonna get?

A room!

What rent?

A rent we can pay!

What rent?

A rent we can pay!

The chants start to form in the children's games.

And a letter to the minister. A petition. Tell him, in case he doesn't know, that they haven't got a house. Inform the king. That's what they did long ago. Maybe the *zaminndar* doesn't know about our suffering. Maybe the lord of the manor is ignorant.

And we'll be in the papers and maybe on television. Or, as Kumar said, maybe not.

'It's here!' cries Giovanni, hugging The Boy Who Won't Speak. 'The bus! Hurry up everyone.' Giovanni grabs hold of Kumar's hand, got a father for now, and together they go door to door, hovel within a hovel, helping everyone close up their front doors of packing crates, of plastic curtains, of tin sheets propped closed with a basalt rock, and come out to the bus.

Then they go to the other courtyards nearby. Just like this one.

The Ter Ruz people from the temporary shelters together with a young girl from the House Movement are leaning out of the bus. Excitement reigned in. The air of expectancy hovers over them too. Like magic.

They've got sheets of cardboard with words written on them, wrapped up in an old *horni* peeping out from behind the bus driver's seat. They welcome the Kan Yolof people shyly and warmly, the bus is their home now, taking the twins in from Sadna Joyna, and stacking the Kan Yolof banners next to theirs.

One woman is bulging with a full-term pregnancy in a tight dress, her ninth, maybe it'll be born today, and she has a selection of the other children with her. They shouldn't miss it, she said.

'It is real. Today is here,' said Kumar. 'Everyone is doing fine. This is just a beginning. Like a warning. A notice we're putting up. Now I'm going to say four things.' He knows how you have to train everyone's attention on what you're saying, because they've got a lot else to concentrate on. And he thinks it would be nice for them all to know about everything that may happen, before it happens. That's what he thinks.

At Senn Mars it's like the orchestra warming up before the opera. Only in real life.

They are signing their letters or putting thumb prints on

162

them, and folding the blue copies up to keep. Fanning themselves with them. Voices like musical instruments. They choose banners.

Jumila has a revelation. Four women all start telling her at once. *We didn't have anywhere to stay. We took the decision to act. We didn't wait for the government. We have taken land. Kowlenn. Law and land into our own hands. We are living on State Land on the mountain slopes just outside Porlwi in Valeé Pitot. Yes now. Already. We are already living there. Of course you can!*

Jumila had never heard anything like it.

Her feet felt equal suddenly. Light. Light. Light. Light.

'There aren't even storm drains,' one of them said. 'But we like it. We are not moving out.' By now Goldilox Soo was listening. She had lived in the woods before, so she just sighed to herself, saying, 'So obvious, isn't it?' And Sadna Joyna overheard, and was seen to dance a quick set of steps.

There was a lot of kissing. Colourful clothing joining and separating. Children pulling women's heads down to kiss them. More buses arriving. Colourful women's clothes and children's T-shirts. More kissing. More people from the mountain flanks coming down, throwing their shiny *horni* over their shoulders. More kissing. More children running around with banners. Yellow red green.

As the first women carrying the main green banner reach the cathedral, the last women with the end red banner are leaving. And every colour of the rainbow in between. Jumila turns around and says to a woman with

163

an armband behind her: 'Is this the *demonstration*?'

'Yes,' she says. 'Yes.'

'Look at my boy,' says Jumila. 'Happy. I've never seen him like that.' The Boy Who Won't Speak was transformed. His eyes glistened. The helplessness he felt, for once, lifted off his young shoulders. Lifted ever so slightly. A playfulness began to glow within him.

'We won't get houses straight away, but we change straight away,' the woman from the House Movement said. 'Look at us. Just look.'

Sadna Joyna caught bits and pieces of speeches. *'Since when an offence to be poor? Whose shame is it anyway?'* Questions, questions, questions.

'Why accept? Why not act?'

Never heard such questions.

'Will you come down on to the streets again?'

'Yes. Yes. Yes.' She heard herself call it out with the others. She was surprised. Then, 'Why not?' she thought. She danced as she shouted. Magnificent movements, fast and inventive. The Queen would have loved to see her now. The Queen had had a house. Their alley.

'How can anyone stand there and tell us we have nowhere to stay on this globe?'

Why hadn't she thought of it that way before. The Queen had.

'What rent will we pay? What rent?'

'A rent we can pay!'

164

'What rent?'
'A rent we can pay.'
Call and response.

Sadna Joyna sees a little boy not more than five years old, crying out, 'A rent we can pay.' He understands these words. It is his everyday worry. At five. Nearby there is an old lady, balancing on the edge of the street, passing by, fetching two young children from kindergarten, who has got riveted to the pavement edge by the demonstration. Her eyes fall on the boy. She sees the boy, sees how his mother has tied her *horni* to his braces, because she's got a babe in arms and a banner to hold, so as not to lose him, and the old lady hears the little boy call, 'A rent we can pay,' as he runs alongside his mother. He cries out with such intensity, an accusation hurled by a child. Tears run down that woman's cheeks.

Just behind Porlwi.

You'd never believe it.

Wind swirls the platinum grass which sucks stories from the mammalian mountain flanks, of a sighing, breathing mother Africa pinioned in exile thus under this basalt rock surrounded by emerald seas where mother whales roam back and forth sighing and breathing and spouting stories to the wintry sun which whispers further stories of the ancestors and their ancestors before them a thousand mothers ago a dozen continents ago into the ears of the seeds of the platinum grass.

Just behind Porlwi. Valleys up in the mountains.
You'd never believe it.
The three of them have decided.

The sun captures the gold in Goldilox Soo's hair and she gives it up to the wind which waves it and then the sun catches her four bits of crate wood that she found and sharpened with a billhook to a sharp point at the one end and the winter wind blows Giovanni who didn't go to school today's cap off and he throws the borrowed hammer with the broken handle tied up with about a hundred yards of string to stop the cap blowing further because children have to. They make no sacrifices. No sacrifices at all. Jumila's shawl with silver thread in it gift-wraps her a present with her four eighteen-inch lengths of quarter-inch steel bars, the ones they use for reinforcing concrete that Rahim got from somewhere. The Boy Who Won't Speak still gives nothing. Only a slightly more haunted look back in his eye. This he bestows. Rahim leaning on his five-foot long crowbar, the same he is, wind or no wind. No superstition in him. As if a full spiritual life doesn't need church or mosque or temple or hymns. Naturally. When a winter whirlwind comes and catches Sadna Joyna's wide green T-shirt material skirt and raises it all around her and she twirls it to make it worse and she hugging her four stakes made from sharpened *lakoklis* tree branches to her heart,

166

elbows to sides, won't let go of them ever ever ever and the whirlwind whirls and twirls her skirt right over her head and ties it in a temporary knot like the cauliflower leaves around the cauliflower at the market only Sadna Joyna gives her body to the wind free she doesn't sell it and she not only gives her body to the wind, but with her elbows to her waist, her hands clutching four stakes between her breasts, her naked hips, thighs, knees, calves, ankles, feet, toes begin to give the world a dance. Make it up invent it take it and give it. The ballet shoes rise up from out of the drum next to what may have been a discarded foetus and get on to her feet and she begins to dance as she has never danced before. Red shoes.

'*Donn li,*' the others cry. 'Give, give, give it, give everything. Give everything you've got!' And she dances and gyrates until her torso lies back, her shoulders inches from the ground, still dancing, then knees to the ground, hips to the wind. The Queen is back watching her. Eating bread and honey. She knew she would dance again. Dance for the love of dance.

Call it four wooden stakes each, and a hammer between them.

'I take thee land. I to thee give myself, land. Just as the sea created life, so the land sustains it.' Thus spake Goldilox Soo.

'We're citizens,' announces Jumila. The others are impressed by this word in the first place, and by its being used as a right to land in the second place.

'Good point,' says Goldilox Soo. She remembered she hasn't got a birth certificate. Such an indelible thought. 'We're people.'

Sadna thinks of the twins, and sees Rahim's she-dog has followed them from when they went past the bare land she lives on in the scar of the race riots on their way from Kan Yolof, so Sadna says: 'We're creatures.'

So this is how the ceremony starts.

The mountain is huge. They stake out three adjacent portions of it, just behind the most recent squatters, whose houses teeter on the mountain slope.

Those without anything *take* very little.

They take enough for a tin room and a six-inches deep pit latrine.

Building their houses was carrying barked eucalyptus poles up the hill on their heads. Building was digging the six-inch holes for each pole to be set in, and constructing the wooden mould for the concrete to be poured around each pole. Four upright poles, with two slanting poles nailed to each diagonally. Four poles with half-cut ends to balance on top of the standing poles and on top of one another. And one across the middle to fix the join of the corrugated-iron to. The two front poles were higher, the back poles lower. Building was carrying second-hand sheets of corrugated-iron up the hill from the hardware shop on their heads. Nailing it down. Putting a tar mixture into the holes in the second-hand corrugated-iron. Building was buying second-hand drums that had been flattened under a road-roller into sheets that could be used as walls and windows and doors. Building was calculating the number of wooden slats for the joins in the flattened iron sheets. Building was picking up nails in Kan Yolof outside the depots.

And then the news came. About caterpillars. Army caterpillars had been flattening the houses by the military road. The government was moving. There was this new law. Five years' prison for squatting. Voted in the National Assembly last year. Now being applied for the first time. Voted unanimously. Squatters are like vermin, they said. And now the demolitions were beginning. The people were being arrested and held in custody. Mrs Ramdin and Mrs Jugroop, two old-age pensioners, held in police cells because of a ten-foot by ten-foot corrugated-iron house on State Land in Plenn Maynan. Held in police cells two days and three nights. Neighbours collected donations to pay the two thousand, two hundred rupees bail. They were charged under the new five years' prison law for illegally occupying the only place in the universe that they had to stay in.

That is when the three of them, Jumila, Sadna and Goldilox Soo, get to be like Kumar and Rahim.

They start to go all over the country to meet other squatters and people without houses. They're everywhere. They all join the House Movement. They meet under a mango tree, they talk. On an old lady's veranda. By the football field.

169

By word of mouth. They find other squatters by recognizing the kind of tin houses. If people are out, they stick invitations on their houses with flour and water glue, just like the government sticks its eviction notices up. They stick their invitations up right there, just next to the eviction notice.

And then comes the day. There we see Rahim and Serge, who's also in the House Movement, in the platinum grass, calling people from out of their shacks with a loudhailer. It's today. There's movement in the platinum grass. Take your rice off the fire. Put on town clothes. Close up house. Down in the streets again.

There are men coming down from the valleys

It's time.

I can hear someone knocking on the door

Women feel the time.
They come down,
Tucking in the strands.

Like a whisper in the wind

No sooner had The Boy Who Won't Speak got back to the upside-down crate with the bras on it, with the Coke and a straw in it for Jumila – she was holding his hand, so pleased to be with him – than a woman from the Women's Movement came up to her. The Boy Who Won't Speak was eating his *gato pima* out of a paper bag.

'Jumila, I knew I'd find you here. Goldilox Soo told me if ever I need bras, where to find you. These are my two workmates at the factory. They've sent us all home, because there's no new orders. The factory may be closing down next week. They can't tell us for sure. Or they won't tell us. You look a bit unwell, Jumila. What's wrong?'

'Nothing much. I'll tell you tonight at the dancing party. You are coming, aren't you? What will you do when the factory closes down?'

'Yes, I'll see you tonight. These two want bras. Juna and Lenn. It's so nice to have a day out of that factory. But it's not worth it when you're scared it's going to close down. We're going to see the Union now. To ask advice. To inform them. I don't know what I'll do. I still owe on my sewing machine. But for Lenn it's worse. She's got two children, and rent to pay. She pays more than half her pay in rent. She'll be out of a house if she doesn't get another job. She doesn't know whether to just leave this one, to be sure she can get another job, before all three hundred and twenty-five of us start looking for work at the same time. And Juna lives with her two old aunts, who're pensioners. What exactly are we supposed to complain to the Union about? What are we supposed exactly to ask the Union to complain about? That we have no means of subsistence? That we

171

have been dispossessed on this earth? That we depend on people we don't know and haven't got any control over? What? See what sizes they take?'

'Do like Sadna Joyna. Right now she's at the court. The Industrial Court. You can't let them get away with it. So, someone closes a factory down, and then your children and you are in this state?' Jumila giving advice, by the bras. The Boy Who Won't Speak is impressed. He has checked on their sizes, and is already finding bras that will fit them.

'What's Sadna doing?'

'She's at the Industrial Court. Not that you can make a complaint by law about someone's factory closing down. You have to find another more minor complaint. Sadna Joyna says you always have to get them on a small point. The big point *they* win. So far. Got to be fought out somewhere else. You can see Sadna Joyna there. She'll be pleased to see you. She's got her case today. Then you can see what it's like, in case you also have to file a complaint. And you can give her confidence as well, if you're there. We'll get you fitted out with bras in no time.'

The Boy Who Won't Speak got them each two or three different kinds of bra to choose from. They discussed prices and each chose two bras, and were busy getting their money out. Nattering on about the factory closing, the size of bra cups, the Industrial Court and the merits of cotton rather than synthetics.

'Yes,' said Jumila's friend. 'Then we can go to the Union after her case is finished.' She was helping the other two get

172

their money out of their purses, counting rupees, when she realised that Jumila was trying to say something to her. Mouthing something. Signalling something. That Jumila's eyes were desperate. That she had gone crooked on her two feet. But she couldn't for the life of her work out what Jumila's message was.

The Boy Who Won't Speak was busy too. He was putting the bras into fifty-cent plastic bags. Head down. Pleased.

Jumila was still trying to signal something. Trying to intimate a threat coming at them all, from behind their backs.

Maybe because they were busy with all that talk, maybe because Jumila was struck dumb herself this time, like The Boy Who Won't Speak and couldn't say anything, maybe because it all happened so quickly.

She didn't manage to get a word of warning in.

Two big plainclothes men, the ones that always do this, just drove up in a jeep, pushed The Boy Who Won't Speak aside roughly so that he fell off the crate, swore at Jumila, '*Verminn, sa bann ti marsan la,*' grabbed all the bras, including the four that had just been bought, and jumped back into the jeep with them, and drove off. They did not manhandle the *public*. Just street merchants.

'But that's not possible,' Jumila's friend shouted. 'You'll have to report this to the police!'

'That is the police,' Jumila said. Her dizziness and weakness had passed.

From time to time Jumila and The Boy Who Won't Speak lost all their bras like that. 'If we go to the police, they'll

173

charge us with selling our wares in a place that we are not allowed to be in. If we don't go, they will just keep the bras. That's the rules.'

'I don't believe it. And you telling us *we* need the Union! What about you? Or are you going to just accept it, accept it just like that.'

'I don't know,' said Jumila. 'I just don't know.'

'You don't look well, Jumila. Take care,' her friend said, and Juna added, 'And, don't worry, we'll come and buy bras from you again. We've still got our money.'

Jumila will have to dip into her savings to replace her stock. It's a bad day today, she says. But at least I've got friends. The only way I get by. Rahim will be furious. At the Lagar Dinor the police have expelled all the sellers of wares so often, that some of them have given up. Now no one can buy loaves of bread to take home anymore. Nor fat-cakes. Nor have a drink of *aluda* just before getting on to the bus. Nor fruit.

It's gone all dingy and quiet and uneasy there now, she muses, as she and The Boy Who Won't Speak sit by their empty crate. Just the public toilets and the odd drug peddlers when evening gets nearer. Women and girls are scared to be there.

And now they'll be cleaning up by the Outer Islands godown. Where all the fishermen sign up for contracts on the fishing banks. Where people ask directions between the two bus stations.

She takes The Boy Who Won't Speak's hand in her own

174

and holds it. She looks at him. There are tears in his eyes, but he bites them back.

The first time he has had tears in his eyes, since what his eyes saw. She hugs him to her, and looks up at the sky. Clouds threaten to squash them.

No sooner had Sadna walked in late, Your Honour, and looked around and sat down thinking about Jumila and Goldilox Soo and them all three trying so hard to get rid of it and that her friend will fetch the twins from the crèche and look after them and the party meeting which seemed unlikely to materialize this afternoon being a farfetched idea in the first place and fetch the twins from her friend and then all off to the dancing party because it was Friday at last and now a one o'clock session of the courts and later the fridge and then the offal lorry and when it would be bedtime then all of a sudden they called out *Joyna the party on the one hand versus something heirs the party on the other hand* and she stood up and the Union lawyer signalled her to go into the box.

She didn't know the difference between a plaintiff and a witness and a defendant but she was here to tell the truth and get her money from that man and get him found to be the guilty party whatever the case especially of killing his wife because she firmly believed it wasn't death by suicide drowning by suicide but death by being driven like in the dream and therefore guilty and also his anyway being guilty of unjust dismissal for kicking her out and have to cough up at punitive rates not to mention for rape.

She also held him responsible in a vague and mistrustful manner for the murders of the Queen and Sheeba.

The labour inspector who was taking her case and the man from the State Law Office representing her sighed in relief now that they knew they wouldn't have to explain to the magistrate where the hell Sadna Joyna, plaintiff, was when her name was called.

The woman from the Union sedately signalled her to come and sit next to her. Three other women Union members had come to be with her for the case. She kissed them each twice. In her most jaunty way. The usher glared at her. Contempt of court. But she didn't notice.

Three other women came in. Looked like factory workers. One of them looking at her, seems to know her. Oh, yes, Goldilox's friend from the Women's Movement. Sadna was pleased to see them. Waved. Like a dance. The usher glared again. Further contempt. She didn't notice again.

'You'll do fine,' said the woman from the Union. 'You have to get them on these small points, remember. Fight it out. Do him for punitive rates, for unjust dismissal. Get the 5,232.49 rupees.' She knew, from long and dreary experience that she had to get Sadna to *concentrate properly*, before they called her to give evidence.

The worker always has to do everything right, otherwise she loses the case, she had explained to Sadna at the meeting of domestic workers. If the boss does wrong things, like lateness, absence, forgetting things, etc., this doesn't matter, and is taken to be a trivial thing. So the Union woman had told Sadna Joyna, who could have told her that herself.

This case is old. Some 170 years old, she told Sadna. From when the British Colonial Office, after taking over from the French, sent a Protector of Slaves out. *In.* She liked saying this *'in'*, the Union woman.

The Abolitionists put pressure on the British Government, and so they sent the Protector out.

When he came out, in, how did the slaves see him?

The same pattern.

Most owners would not give permission for slaves to go and see the Protector.

The Protector took the side of the owners most of the time.

In the face of the injustice of slavery itself, an injustice so gross, what do slaves reasonably come forward to report? They could not report *the fact that they were slaves*, she explained. Nor can you. She was trying to concentrate Sadna Joyna's mind.

You can't put in general complaints, she had said to Sadna Joyna.

Sadna can't say she had no other way of staying alive, for example. She can't say she had no other house to live in.

And so she had to do just as those slaves had to do and did. They would bring up those things, those points, however minor, that they thought may just be won, given their knowledge that the legal system actually keeps them as slaves. They could try protesting to the Protector of Slaves for being punished for protesting against Sunday work, protesting to the Protector of Slaves for being punished for going to see the Protector of Slaves, protesting to the Protector of Slaves for getting punished for trying to prevent the beating of another slave or for asking for a day off, protesting to the Protector of Slaves for being punished for not beating another slave enough, or protesting to the Protector of Slaves for being punished for stealing food. You couldn't win on complaining about the *slavery*. She had a point.

So Sadna Joyna was protesting to the Magistrate at the Industrial Court, the Protector of Workers, for not being given *severance allowance*. Everybody knows those two words. Severance allowance. Like for getting a limb cut off. And it being permitted. She couldn't complain about wage slavery. Even rape and murder were too difficult to win on.

So too had the Protector of Immigrants dealt with the complaints of generations of women from India, the woman from the Union said.

Immigrants who had had to find a specific, often apparently minor point on which to complain. You couldn't win on the point of being reduced to indenture.

And yet it must be done. Complaints must be made. The Union meeting had convinced Sadna.

Sadna Joyna knew. Fight them on the small points,

178

where you can. Do them for a rupee cheated on piece rates. And fight them on the big issues too. Some other place and time. That's what they were waiting for. The place and the time.

On 5th June, 1995 what happened?

Many things, no doubt.

Come on, Mrs or is it Miss Joyna? What happened in relation to your employment? That's what we're here for.

Perhaps you mean I lost my boss that day?

Mrs Joyna, I am after all your counsel. There's no need to ask me questions.

My what?

Lawyer, barrister. Yes, indeed your employer passed away.

No, she didn't not just like that she didn't pass away not just like that.

Speak to the magistrate, please Mrs or is it Miss Joyna?

But, he's not speaking to me.

Mrs (resigned now to this appellation) Joyna, I am as I have already mentioned your counsel. You can trust me. Take my advice. Address your replies to the magistrate, using the words 'Your Honour'.

You were saying that she passed away.

No, Your Honour, not just like that, she didn't. It was not natural causes.

Look at the magistrate, please.

The magistrate interrupted at this point to say: 'The Coroner will decide this matter. Go on.'

She had no idea what they were talking about.

Your boss, who passed away, was she married to someone?

Yes, Your Honour.

Look at the magistrate, please.

To whom was she married?

To her husband, sir.

And who is the man who was her husband when she was alive?

The police chief, Your Honour. In charge of the Drug Squad.

Can you see him in this court?

Yes, he's there on the other side.

The magistrate again interrupted to say: 'This is not a criminal matter, so counsel need not have his client identify this respondent. He is known to the court.'

Yes, Your Honour. Sorry Your Honour. I produce a certified copy of the marriage certificate. Marriage took place between the defendant and his deceased spouse. Date 1974. Community of property. I think this establishes the Latin Latin Latin.

When did you start working for your ex-employer, Mrs or is it Miss (doubt has crept in again) Joyna?

You can call me Mrs, Your Honour. (Here she wasn't sure if she was supposed to say Your Honour, because it certainly didn't sound right because he didn't call her anything.)

Beginning of 1994.

Were you in continuous service?

Yes, Your Honour.

Magistrate: 'Does your client know what continuous service means?'

I never stopped working there, Your Honour. Just public holidays and sick leave. I never got my local leave.

We'll come to that, Mrs Joyna.

Instead of reporting that he beat his wife the day before she committed suicide. Instead of reporting that he raped Sadna, in front of his wife. Instead of reporting how he had imprisoned his wife, Rita. Instead of reporting all this. She was reduced to reporting the failure to pay severance allowance.

Instead of reporting that she was in a position of extreme weakness relative to any employer. Especially this one. Instead of reporting the existence of her wage slavery, she was reduced to reporting the failure to pay severance allowance.

She was determined to win her case.

Choose a point, and win it in the meantime, she said to herself again and again.

'What socialist party ever owned a dog?'

Well their party did.

That's what Sadna, Jumila and Goldilox Soo first liked about the party. Before they ever thought of coming to a meeting. Not the dog himself (that would come later), but the fact that the party had one.

That's why they agreed to come to their first meeting.

Before that, they just knew some party members through the House Movement or the Union or the Women's Movement.

They asked two of the members, Alex and Rajen, how a party could have a dog.

'We didn't want to own a dog. One thing a party doesn't need is a dog,' said Alex.

'It was never a decision that came up in a branch nor was it ever transmitted to the central committee or anything. But there you have it, we own a dog,' added Rajen.

'How did you get him?'

'He got kicked out of the brothel. There's this brothel on State Land just down the road. A brothel that does on-premises services and catch-a-taxi to the Moonbay Hotel services too. And one thing a brothel can't stand is a bad dog. And this dog is a bad dog. Wherever they do their services, they don't like bad dogs.'

None of the three women had ever heard such open references to a brothel in mixed company. Everyone pretended they didn't exist, or if they did, that they weren't frequented by ordinary humans, but perhaps by tourists or Martians or someone.

'The dog would follow clients to the bus stop on the main road and stand next to them like an 'I was at the brothel' sign.

'Clients would kick him in the ribs, then try to ignore him, and then kick him in the ribs again.

'But the damage was done. A dog has the power to keep clients away. The fear of god doesn't. Nor do acts of god. Even cyclones can't stop clients turning up. Clients, as generations of prostitutes have complained from the Semino to this brothel, appear immediately a Class III warning is taken off. There they are, queuing up. That's what the girls who work there can't believe. Right after a cyclone, they say. Cyclones don't discourage clients. Nor do the priests and parsons. The police sometimes *try* to. They all try, but nothing doing.

'But a dog has the power to discourage them.

'Specially a puppy that hangs on to a client's right leg, with his two front paws crossed around this client's leg, and does rude movements mimicking what they're about to do or have just done. This they can't stand.

'No one knows if he learnt this from what he saw at the brothel or if it was some particular behavioural disorder of this dog. But be that as it may, that's what he would do to clients' legs at the bus stop, right in front of everyone. Roger them. Just as if to tell everyone and even show everyone.

'This is one thing brothel clients do not like. Ridicule. Public ridicule.'

He looks like the dog that guards the River Styx, only with just the one head.

He is black. But when they got him he was only black where there was hair, but mainly there wasn't any hair left because of the mange, so he was left pink and mangy. As though clients even left the mange there. So you could catch even mange there. Not just the clap. Not just Aids. But mange as well.

He smelt like old socks. Again, no one knew whether the smell somehow came from the brothel which also smelt of old socks or if it was honest-to-goodness dog smell.

'Now brothel clients have a delicate equilibrium. They're persistent, but there are limits. And he, this dog, could drive any brothel client's psychological equilibrium into the realms of rabid heebie-jeebies.

'As though his transmogrified sins and reified evil deeds and hidden inside monsters had all got out, got set loose, escaped into the outside objective world, so as to torment him, humiliate him and make him look stupid.

'Roger his leg.

'You couldn't pretend nothing was happening or even that you didn't know the dog under such circumstances. Something was happening and the dog obviously knew you because dogs don't tell lies about these things. And since he was known to hang out by the brothel, the entire public gathering at the bus stop had thus been informed that you had just come from the brothel. You started to feel as though you smelt of the brothel and began to lift your arm up and sniff. You got scared to go directly home. And you went and bought aftershave. And you kept checking he wasn't still following you when you got to your home stretch.

'The only thing you could do to prevent all this humiliation and unease, was to stop coming to the brothel. To that brothel anyway. No other way around the hell hound.

'You were done. You gave up. You stayed away.

'Clients never came back.

'So the brothel-keepers, foul, lazy pimps with their violent ways, beat the hell out of the dog to get him to move right out of the brothel. They raised their hands to him, and their boots, and switches and sticks. They even threw stones at him. And then rocks. Anything to get rid of him. But he loved the brothel. He had no other home anyway. So he tried to stay. But these brothel-keepers are vicious and he, the dog, sensed their violence knew no bounds. And he was right. Especially when business was involved.'

So that when, stubborn as he was, he turned up at the party headquarters, party members naturally tried to kick him out. But their party, however militant they were and are, in relation to the special police, none of them could beat a dog. And certainly they could never beat a dog more than a pack of brothel-keepers could. And they knew how much they would have to beat that dog to get rid of him.

And so they gave up.

And took him in.

Reluctantly.

They gave him food scraps and didn't kick him out.

Lead poisoned he was, from the battery factory, thin as a rake, and this hairlessness an affront.

He offered his services as a watchdog.

'He made it clear he had moved in and he wasn't moving out. Then he started barking at any new recruit that came along. Because we didn't beat him, he loved us. He proved it by barking at all newcomers. Now this is bad news for a political party, because political parties like to get new members. Keeping new recruits out, this was nearly as bad as keeping brothel clients from a brothel.'

So the party decided to make a nice dog out of him.

One member grabbed a hold of him and another showered him in the shower cubicle and shampooed him. Dried him with a hairdryer. Of course, this did nothing for his hairlessness. But the smell, his own inimitable smell came back more or less immediately.

They knew he was only a puppy because his balls hadn't even started to dangle yet. Still stuck to his bum like a pair of socks rolled up.

They never gave him a name consciously. One day a name just got stuck to him, really stuck, like his balls to his bottom. He got called Beauty. A boy dog called Beauty. Only, when he was naughty he was called The Beast.

One day Alex and Rajen ordered a taxi without a regular license, asked him to drive right in, asked if a dog could get into the boot. He said 'how much' and they decided on the price. When they got to the MSCPA to get the medicine for the mange, at the counter there was this bleak officer who said, 'And what's your dog called, Sir?' and after an embarrassing silence, Alex said: 'He is called Beauty.'

'That dog?' he said.

'Yes,' they both said, 'this dog. He's ours and he's called Beauty.' Some people in the queue were heard to snigger, but the looks they got from Alex and Rajen just shut them right up. 'Any objection?'

Soon in the headquarters' messages book, alongside messages of the type *'Been invited by Porlwi Youth Group to send speaker to forum next Tuesday at the Social Centre, phone 212–3346 after 6 p.m.'*, or *'Don't miss the TV news, strike in South Korea'*, *'PM holding special press conference tomorrow Vagji Hall eleven'*, they started to get more and more messages of another type: *'Bought and cooked chicken liver for Beauty; it's in the covered dekti'* or *'Couldn't catch Beauty to tie him up on his running chain this morning'*, and *'Beauty followed me right on to the Rose-Hill transport bus, and the conductor said is that your dog? And after some hesitation, I felt I couldn't disown him, I could already see the conductor preparing a kick in his direction: Yes, he is my dog. Thank you. Did I do the right thing?'*

Then there was the mange medicine saga, putting it on every eight days, until he built up this shiny coat. He started to run just like a slim race horse. Chasing members' bicycles, motorbikes, cars, following members to the bus stop. And by the time his balls were swinging, he could listen to two commands: *'Come here at once'* and *'Sit'*. He could also offer himself up to his running chain every morning at about seven. He got trained by a party member who worked at Domaine les Pailles where he was a groom by profession. He just treated Beauty like any horse after it's come over by sea. 'This dog is as dislocated and distressed as a horse over from South Africa,' he said. 'Needs to be talked to. Will learn to be a good dog in no time.'

Beauty was an excellent security check for the party. He was a way of judging new members. How do they relate to Beauty? This was how Sadna Joyna and Goldilox Soo and Jumila were immediately accepted. Beauty thought they were the most marvellous newcomers ever to set foot into headquarters, and they reciprocated.

No one knows why.

Nothing could kill Beauty either. No one expected him to last. Thought he was a temporary problem.

Other dogs died as puppies in road accidents. But Beauty crossed at the Zebra Crossing. In a one mile radius, all other dogs lost weight from the lead poisoning, and got thinner and thinner, then started to walk sideways, then started having fits, epileptic fits, then died. But Beauty was fit as a fiddle. Yet other dogs got the dog enteritis, vomited blood and died within days. Or the worms that eat their hearts. Others were lost at night. Gone off on a dog-marriage party, never to return. Some got drowned when the river came down in cyclones.

But not Beauty.

Only once did he get sick. Rajen said: 'This dog's going to die. I'll take him to the vet, in case other members think there may have been hope. But he looks a goner to me.'

On the way there, Rajen tells, he started to pick up in the

car he had borrowed for the trip. Started lifting his head up and sniffing at every turn in the road. By the time he got to the hospital queue, he was attacking other sick dogs there, and Rajen wondered why he had brought him. Before going in to consult, he got his name checked, and by the time he got his injection, he was just fine.

He was skinny. Scruffy. Ugly. But he represented a defiance against society. A defiance against history. A defiance against nature. He was life personified. Like weeds. Tenacious. In good faith. Indestructible.

'Any party that can adopt a dog like Beauty has got a future,' they said. Goldilox Soo said it. Sadna and Jumila agreed.

They made it. A quiet hush, and warm looks. Smiles and calm and attentiveness. All three were at ease. Work over and children safe in the hands of others. Beauty sat just behind their bench, putting his paw on it. Next to their bottoms.

'Brief call for reports about anything going on where you live, in your neighbourhoods?' said the woman member who was presiding. 'Brief and to the point. If your report includes something that is more a rumour than information, please also add what you did to check on it, or to dispel it. If you don't add this, don't bother to tell it. We don't want rumours repeated, please. Remember: a new kind of movement.'

This introduction means Sadna will have to prepare to talk just in case Goldilox Soo doesn't say anything because Jumila probably won't be in a fit state to say anything about them staking out their land and should she ask if they've heard of bulldozers threatening more flattening and worse still maybe if no one else says it she'll have to tell of the rumours and about the preparing of acid vials in light bulbs that's going on and the petrol bombs in half-jacks and the sharpening, sharpening the pangas and sabre knives on the circular stone, since you're supposed to tell rumours at a party meeting, but did I do anything to dispel them? And the case went well. He is a guilty party even though they said it's only a civil case. He's not very civil. Civil Hospital tonight to see the offal man, can't say that.

'Hope the fridge is all right,' thought Goldilox Soo. 'I, who have never had the use of a fridge before, now use it as a temporary abode for my friend's lost foetus. A chilly purgatory. Let alone a microwave.'

'Drains in Sité Malerb blocked and causing a stench. What to do.'

Wait her turn. Concern. The Queen had told Sadna of the race riots. There's the scar by Rahim's house, she knew it. She felt in her bones, especially the bones of her ankles, just where the shackles would have been, that they're coming back again with the acid and the petrol and the grindstone. How would she ever dance again then?

190

Not coming back by themselves though. They wouldn't be coming back by themselves. Spirits don't. 'I am guilty of bringing them back. I and you and you, too. We ourselves. The future victims. By our omissions. Except that right here, right now, we are acting. Or rather beginning to act. Now that I am here. Now that I am poised to act. But I must be vigilant. I mustn't miss the moment to speak, to speak up, to speak out. Moments are easy to miss.'

'Group of cane labourers in Klini asking for a local meeting about politics and work conditions.' Details. Someone delegated. Anyone else want to arrange to go?

'Love to,' thought Sadna. 'Another time, on one of my off days.' She knew a bit about labour law now, and the Industrial Court.

'Petitions are back from the two villages in the north that hadn't submitted theirs yet, it's about the water-pollution problem.'

'Good, that means we can deliver them to the Minister of the Environment. Need to make an appointment if we want to actually see him? Who would like to go? Official delegates? Other people present?'

'Just like that,' thought Jumila. 'How do they know that they can just do all these things? How come other people don't know? That's what a party is? A perpetual permit. You don't have to ask permission from anyone. Take your rights. Take them. Maybe that's it. Who knows?'

'Further information?' the woman member presiding asked.

'Must try to act. To think and act. To prevent and then to create. But will I get the words out when my turn comes? Will I know when it comes?' thought Sadna.' Have I got the persistence? Do I want to avoid the worst and create the best? Together with others.

'Or do I shirk. I catch myself these days doing it, being the perpetrator of the stuff that acid and petrol and pangas are made of. I caught myself the other day, looking in the mirror at the false orthopedic joints section, and thinking slavethoughts again. Strong young female "Mozambique" no disease not yet produced offspring. Strong Malabar man. I think of the twins. Two sprung off. Or out. Two hundred *pyas* or four hunting guns with powder keg. Submit or kill yourself, Sadna, the slavethought comes again. Your two choices. Submit. Or if not, suicide. *Mo zis enn ti malbar mwa.* I'm just a little coolie. *Little*, so *little* it's not worth your while hitting me. So submitted, you can't see me. *Malbar*, so you feel justified in insulting me, after all she calls herself it. *Malbar*. *Malbar*. *Malbar*. *Ti Malbar*. Healthy. *Lascarinn* pregnant possibly twins three hundred *pyas*. What shall I tell the little ones as they're born? "You'll always be little. But cower to make yourself smaller." I catch myself. "Smaller than what? Than everybody else, of course. Be obsequious. Stay, at most, resentful. You can sulk. That, they don't notice. And with the smell of revenge trapped by your necessary cowardice rising around you, smoulder, twins, smoulder. For your revenge is petty. I catch myself telling them slavetalk. Never say the word change, twins, I catch myself saying. Because it has the most awful consequences. Never say the word equality. They don't like it. It alone reminds them of the part of the French revolution they don't celebrate with big dinners on 14th July. Classify yourself as well, like an animal, and classify your fellow creatures, by race of course, and when you're allowed one, by religion, by imagined ancestors and invented castes. It appeases their desire to starve you, it appeases your desire to rise up, it feeds your vile circular desire to get stuck in the past, it appeases their desire to hit you.

'This is what the light bulbs full of balancing acid are made of. This is what the half-jacks of petrol are made of. This is what the grinding stone going round and round is made of. Slugs and snails and puppy dogs' tails. Finger of birthstrangled babe ditch delivered. Where did they put the birthstrangled babe when they chopped the finger off? Was it easy to get rid of? Puppy dog's tails. Sheeba's big tail and her seven pairs of hairy tits.

'Whenever I think of a dog getting killed I think of my mother the Queen as though she and Sheeba were one. Animals up to dignity or humans down to animality. Thought and speech the only difference. Represent the world. Human speech.'

'I have two things to say.' She said the words.

She is managing to open her mouth.

With some difficulty.

'Some people. Some people on the mountain flanks where we three live, Goldilox Soo, Jumila and myself, some people, who live near us are preparing weapons, I. Know two of them, I. Think they are involved in some communal preparations, they. Used to walk around with pangas at the height of the Naked Midnight Man scare. The same people, now. They spread rumours about "the others". "The others", they say, are preparing. We, they say, must too. They talk about "them" and "us" when they are talking about their own neighbours, their own workmates. It is frightening. That's the one thing that I.

'The other thing. My friend's got this leaflet from the school. The government school. Here it is. Maybe you would like to read it out, or to keep it in a file here.'

And so it was that she said the things she had to say. She said the things the three of them had decided to say.

Then, quite unexpectedly, Jumila said she had something to say. Sadna and Goldilox gulped. They hoped she wasn't going to tell about the plastic bag in the freezer. No. Please, don't. You never know with an angry woman, they thought.

'It's about the police. They just took all my wares again today. I was by the Millers' Group of Companies godown, with my son, adoptive son, and these two plainclothes men came and took everything. Again. I'm a seller of wares.'

Then Sadna, Jumila and Goldilox could concentrate on what everybody else was saying. Precise things.

Understanding. In their understanding. Within their grasp. Making things change with their own hands.

There were no momentous decisions.

Afterwards Jumila would say how glad she was she had gone. Victory. In *going*, she said. Even though she had still been feeling weak and light-headed. There was just enough sharing of information and ideas that you didn't feel like history's sitting duck, she said.

'Let's all three go up. The hurly-burly's done.' They were standing near the canal, outside the Millers' Group of Companies building. The day's heat was receding, the rain that had never really come, except for a brief moment, was still hanging like a possibility in the air.

Sadna Joyna always missed the Queen at this hour in Porlwi, when the prostitutes became more noticeable and the banana sellers were in their alleyways and hidden homes. She almost looked out for Sheeba. The office workers had already gone home. The last of the skilled workers with their tin suitcases in one hand, bent their heads down and, in turn, hurried home. She felt a fear of losing someone or something.

She wanted the three of them to stay together. 'All three,' she said again.

So they all went to the service entrance, on the side. All three of them together. It had just got dark and peaceful outside. Suddenly bright fluorescent light on the inside. Like an assault.

Jumila lost her nerve. 'What will we say if they see us?' Jumila started.

'We'll say I left something upstairs and I've come back to fetch it.'

'What if they ask what it is you've left? What if they say they have to do a security check on what it is? What if they've already found out and are lying in wait for us? What if . . .?' Jumila went on.

'What if! What If! What if! Don't be negative,' Sadna helped with this answer. And she went on: 'How can we concentrate on changing the world, when we have to get rid of foetuses on the quiet, and stay out of the way of Goldilox Soo's bosses, of watchmen, of policemen, of god knows who else?' She was getting cross again. 'Who's the security guard? Know him, Goldilox Soo?'

'Oh, it's the Gardkwik company. Sister company to Klinnkwik. Could be anyone. *Oh, there he is.*'

They walked over to him. He was watching the silent televisions. He started.

'I left something in the messroom, so we're going up to fetch it. Want to come along?'

'No, I have to stay here. Go along up.'

'So silly of me. I clean forgot. Must have been when I was cleaning the messroom.'

'Thanks,' she added.

'All three of you have to go up?'

'Why not?'

'OK.'

Goldilox Soo opens the fridge door.

They peer in.

'It's not in there,' says Jumila, still attached to the thing somehow. Until disposed of.

'Don't be silly, Jumila, I put it in the freezer. Open the freezer door, and take it out.'

She opens the freezer door, it's one of those that's inside the fridge itself.

And the freezer was bare.

Someone had stolen it. Must have thought it was frozen meat.

'Steal so much around here, they steal dead foetuses.'

Jumila was concerned. She felt it like an assault. 'Who's taken it, Goldilox Soo? What's happened to it?'

When they got downstairs, the Gardkwik man wasn't at the televisions anymore.

'He must be outside,' Golidlox Soo said. Just outside the service entrance, they found him, sitting on the wall with his stick. A dog was trying to befriend him by lying close by.

'Find it?' he asked.

She said, 'No. Stolen.'

*

He said, 'Have you got five minutes for a story?' He saw them hesitate. 'It's about stealing things.'

'Of course,' Goldilox Soo said.

They were still thinking about what had happened, and whether there was danger in it or not. They sat on the wall next to his sentry post at the side of the Millers' Group of Companies building. He told them a very old story.

This is the story he told them.

'One day there was a woman in her house with her paramour. Her husband had set off from home on a journey the night before without saying exactly when he would come back. Early in the morning, the cock crowed, and the woman heard a knock at the door. She called out: "Who's there?"

'Her husband replied, "It's me."

'So the woman said to her paramour, "Hurry up, get into that huge jar in the corner of the room."

'He went and hid.

'As soon as the woman opened the door, her husband asked if there was already water on the boil for coffee. She replied, "I'm putting it on right now; but how come you're back so soon?"

' "I met the person I was going to visit on the way there, so I came right back, that's all."

'No sooner had the water boiled, than the woman poured it into the coffee pot. The rest of the boiling water – I have no idea what got into her – you know what she went and did with it? She poured it into the huge jar where her paramour was hiding.

'Poor sod. He never said another word. The boiling water cooked him, he went stiff and pegged. He died with his mouth half open as if he was laughing.

'Later that morning, as soon as her husband had gone to get orders for his work, she said to her paramour, "Hurry up, he's gone, get out of here before he comes back again."

'Her paramour did not budge.

'"Hurry up! For Christ's sake, get a move on!

'"What? You grin like that when I speak to you!"

'When he wouldn't stop grinning, she grabbed him by his hair, pulled him out of the jar. Only then did she realize that he was dead.

'"Good god, now what! What am I to do with a dead body in my house?"

'She thought and thought and thought. Then she remembered. There was an old donkey that used to wander around the yard. She took the dead body and sat it up on the donkey's back and tied it on to the donkey with some old rope. Then she let the donkey out of the yard.

'The donkey trotted off. He made straight for the maize fields of a big planter. The donkey just chewed and chewed the mealies. He was only used to *syendan* grass. While he was chewing away, the planter's wife came out and saw a man on a donkey, letting his donkey eat her maize.

'"Hello! Hello! Hello! What's this then? Are you going to let that creature of yours eat all my maize? And you sitting on top of him all the while? Can't you do something about it instead?"

'The man didn't reply. He just went on grinning.

' "What's the meaning of this! I talk to you politely and you just make a fool of me like that."

'The woman was furious, so she called out loudly for her husband to come.

'The planter came along with a big stick. His wife said: "You won't believe this. I've spoken to this man, asked him to stop his animal from eating our maize, and all he does is make fun of me, grin at me."

'The husband started to beat the man on the donkey up. Thud! The man fell down off the donkey. The man saw this and said: "Oh Lord. Lord, dear wife, what have we done. We have killed a man. What can we do now?"

'The wife thought about their predicament, and said: "Don't be afraid. I've got an idea."

'She went and picked up a bundle of old clothes and tied the dead man up in the bundle of clothes. She carried her bundle of clothes down towards the river. Then she pretended she had forgotten the soap at home, and put the bundle down. And ran off to fetch the soap.

'Thieves turned up on the spot, grabbed the bundle and ran off with it.

'This was how the woman got out of trouble.

'There's so much thieving around, they'll even steal dead people. And that's the end of my story.'

*

200

By the way, he said, still laughing, 'Where did you leave it?'

Goldilox Soo said, 'Oh, to be honest, I was using the fridge. The Millers' fridge. We aren't supposed to. I left something in the fridge. In the freezer, in fact.' Then she added, flippantly, so that he wouldn't take matters any further, 'Serves me right, I suppose.'

'Oh, well. Why didn't you say so! I could have told you. No need to worry. The light in the fridge wasn't working, so the technicians came to fix it. They had to switch the fridge off – it was something wrong with the wiring – so they took everything out. They haven't finished the job. The frozen stuff is in a styrofoam box with ice in it, till morning. It's on the table in the messroom. You go get your stuff. On your own though, this time. Don't want to take any risks. Shouldn't have let all three of you up the first time. You know what Gardkwik are like, you work for Klinnkwik. Sister companies.'

Goldilox Soo nodded.

She went in again.

This time, instead of going straight up in the lift – either lift – she was drawn round to the foyer. To the televisions. Playing to no one now. 'The Mauritian Miracle' on three. News on the other two. New newscaster. Less tired. Same child. Repeat some bits of the news all day. And then a boat capsizing. Illegal immigrants, it looked like. She guessed it must be somewhere near Italy.

Then she went on up.

Fetch it from the styrofoam box. All efficiency now. A practical matter.

She came down five minutes later with the Priba Paradise bag, in which there was the Air Islands Duty Free bag, in which there was a blue one-rupee plastic bag in which there was Jumila's foetus.

The security guard looked up as Goldilox Soo got back and said to all three of them, 'The police say they have been called in from holiday. No leave given as from tonight. Everyone on call. I'm nervous. We're all on our own you know. They're all on stand-by, the police. Even the ones in training have been told to be ready for duty at a minute's notice. I tell you, they're expecting something. *Trouble*. Some kind of trouble. And since it's not an invasion, it must be from the inside. From us.'

'Maybe the police are helping cause something, if you ask me,' said Goldilox Soo. 'A real inside job.'

'Maybe,' he said. 'But there's nothing we can do about it.'

Goldilox Soo looked at him as he spoke. It was as if he was seeing the *trouble* on the silent televisions in the foyer. Just this slight nervousness had managed to get into him. He touched his company cap too often with one hand, and looked at his stick in his other hand.

'Goodnight,' they all said.

Goldilox Soo was still clutching the plastic bag. They set off up into the slopes of the mountains around Porlwi. On foot.

Jumila, one foot light, one foot heavy, mumbled something. Sadna didn't hear her.

Goldilox Soo took it that she was relieved that it hadn't been stolen before they'd got rid of it.

'*Trouble*,' Goldilox Soo said aloud. 'Do you think we can do anything about it now anyway?'

'At least we can face up to it,' Sadna Joyna announced, 'instead of just suffering it.'

'I don't see why we can't try and prevent it,' said Jumila. Of all people.

'I'll carry it,' she added, putting her hand out to take the bag swinging in Goldilox Soo's hand.

One foot light, one foot heavy, the bag took on the rhythm of Jumila's stride.

'No, Jumila, no more housework. The cooking's done, the battle's nearly won,' said Sadna. 'You just lie down on this mat and relax.'

Sadna straightened out a rolled-up grass mat.

'On your tummy first. It's massage time. That's right.'

The foetus was hanging on the same hook it had hung on that morning when Jumila was equalizing the lay of the land. So the red ants wouldn't find it. It was a neutral presence to them now. They were used to it. Not so scared of it anymore. They knew they could get it to the offal lorry after the dancing party. Still had to watch out for the red ants though. 'You have to watch babies' belly buttons when they're first born for red ants as well,' Sadna said.

Giovanni was bathed and sitting on the bed watching television, '*Questions pour un champion*'. 'Questions for a mushroom,' he called it, laughing. He had his hands each on top of one of the twins' heads. They were bathed and powdered and asleep next to him, already fed, sucking their thumbs. The Boy Who Won't Speak had bathed and had intimated that he wanted to sew again, but Jumila had told him it was a time of rest. 'You are the nicest child in the universe,' she said to him. 'Come and give me a hug.' She had had to teach him to hug again. Slowly, she had said, 'Take this hand, and put it here, and this one here, and I hold you like this, and we squeeze, and isn't that nice. It's all cuddly, and warm. See?' For months he hadn't been convinced. But she had persevered, and he had learned again. Learned to hug again.

Now she said to him, 'We are having a ceremony around the meal. A sort of system. Because we have had a difficult day. You probably noticed. Women's matters. And we are in a political party now. You can also be, when you're of age. Ask Rahim one day.' She sometimes pretended it was natural that he would just speak one day. 'You know a damn sight more about life than most. At the meeting, they say that a party is everyone's ideas put together and worked out. That means yours too. Think about that, Tibye. And by the way, you're called Tibye from now on, not The Boy Who Won't Speak. Then if you want to, you can. Can speak, I mean. You just see for yourself.' Because he didn't talk back, you could explain everything to him in detail. 'And then, we have the dance to go to. You'll like that. You can watch us all dancing. Maybe after the dance, and after a few weeks have passed, you'll want to talk.'

All three women had bathed themselves at their respective houses. Standing in a tin bath, pouring warm water from a *dekti* over themselves with a green-pea tin that someone converted by putting a nice handle on it. And put on clean clothes. But not smart clothes.

Jumila was lying down. She had finished fussing around with her dhall, the rice was cooked, the cauliflower and potato curried, and the sardine chutney prepared, with lots of chillies in it.

She was lying down as Sadna had told her to, on her tummy. Sadna sat astride her, on her buttocks, and massaged her shoulders and arms and back. On and on. Goldilox Soo massaged her legs, the heavy one and the light one, one by one, thighs and then calves.

Slowly Jumila came back into her own. Like her body and mind had separated and were reuniting.

Then they turned her over, and Sadna gently rubbed her tummy, consoling it for its loss. And Goldilox Soo massaged her feet.

Sadna said: 'I'll teach you to dance, Jumila, a special dance for your special legs.'

Then they got up. Sadna got a half-jack with two tots of rum in it out of the twins' bag of things. They shared it three ways.

Then they gave Giovanni and The Boy Who Won't Speak their rice and dhall, their curry and chutney, saying, 'There you are, Giovanni and Tibye.'

Jumila and Sadna sat on the bed and Goldilox Soo sat on the only chair.

'Well, we're saying goodbye to your pregnancy. Saying goodbye properly. You're not just all on your own. We're not being surreptitious. It's not all in secret. Not as if we're in the wrong. It's natural, Jumila. It's normal. It's innocent. We'll try and make it as easy as if you chose to do it yourself.' This was Sadna speaking.

'And,' said Jumila, surprising them, 'hello to new things. I think that meeting was interesting. Everyone had something special to say. Even me. Even I did. My sadness will pass. With a bit of help from my friends,' and she looked at them for a long time. 'And we are moving on to all manner of new things.'

'But maybe it's too late now. Things are already falling apart. Unless we're lucky.' That was Goldilox Soo, naturally.

The food tasted sublime.

'It's that recipe I told you about. I inherited it,' said Jumila. 'Thank you for making my house come back to life by your auspicious presences.'

'How did you make this dhall?'

'Oh, it isn't difficult. Just like we all do, except there's dhall plus red and black lentils, the onions have to be over-browned, and then there's some yoghurt, about a cupful. And I nearly forgot, instead of turmeric, I used some garam masala, fried very slightly.'

'Hurry up, it's time to go to the party. Nani's expecting us.'

They rolled up two grass mats for Giovanni and Tibye and Tibye folded up a blanket for the twins. Later on, when the children were tired, they would curl up in rows on the floor in Nani's bedroom, while the women have their party in the other room.

Sadna put on her little red shoes. Just when everyone else took their shoes and sandals off and left them at the door. These were not the little-girl red shoes of her child-hood, dancing for the Queen, dancing at the *L'Alliance Française*, dancing to forget the bananas, dancing to forget the alleyway, dancing to forget the Semino, dancing to dream. These were her own homemade woman's red shoes. These weren't the cast-off shoes of a dead Mrs Blignault but her own shoes. These weren't the shoes of any nation, of any community, these were not the shoes of any religion. These were her shoes and could be anyone's shoes for the making, everyone's shoes for the learning how to make your own shoes. The shoes of life in the past, re-learned in the present, and handed by word of mouth, down to the future. But to learn to dance you have to dance yourself.

No one can do it for you.

There was something about Sadna that night when she danced that brought the Queen deep inside her back out and Sheeba with her seven pairs of hairy tits as well. These were things that she'd shut in just as tight as she had shut in the red ballet shoes when she shoved them into the rubbish drum, squashed in beside what may have been a thrown-away foetus. She let them out. Let them all hang out. She danced of the Orient meeting the Occident, of the sun meeting the moon, of the sea meeting the land, of the horizon meeting the sky, of human meeting animal, of mother meeting twins in her loins, fathered by the mountain and the reef, she danced for the healer healing the sick, for the old initiating the young, for the living meeting the dead. She danced for Jumila's lost child.

Her beauty was unbeknown to her.

Then Goldilox Soo stood up. In her hands was a dark doll. Half a twin, she danced for the other half, Tizan Tronsonez. They were one when they were orphaned. Child-mothered. The doll became the child and then the mother. Invaded. Impregnated, her tummy swelled out in the dance. Digging, digging, trying to hide a first foetus. Found out. Ejected. Sent to the woods in the north. Impregnated mysteriously.

The doll now Giovanni born. Now a witch who cared for them. Now they were saved by Sara's husband looking for a companion for his alcoholic wife.

And then Goldilox Soo rose in a memory dance to Sara, resuscitating her from the burnt charcoal doll to the flesh and blood Sara, and people said they smelt incense and saw soft cotton cloth and on their palates came the taste of Bombay sweets just watching her dancing like that. Her halo lit the entire dark shack. No dead saints stultified in old buildings but new now living haloes of hair. She had moved into Sara's henna.

And then Jumila got rid of the devils in her, dancing one light foot, one heavy foot, one foot light, one foot heavy, the live child she had lost who was with her past husband and The Boy Who Won't Speak and the dead foetus. She danced for her child-sweetheart adult-sweetheart same man. She danced for her forced marriage and forced pregnancy. She danced against the big brothers. She took an empty two-litre Fanta bottle and half-filled it with tap water and balanced it on her head and did the dance of the woman with the body that can do anything wonderful so long as the head is poised and thinking, faster and faster wilder and wilder lower and lower the others playing the *ravann* faster hitting the *dolok* louder tapping the fork on the *catora* quicker singing singing chorusing calling chorusing calling

*

Suddenly she began to dance against the deeper pulse beat in things, against the shackles still on her one foot heavy one foot light, evening out her weight now, her legs in equilibrium now, scarf flying lilting beside her, one foot less heavy one foot less light, and she danced against the past for taking little children, holding them down and taking oaths to god in their names.

Give, she danced, give unto the children the freedom to fly, and her arms light and equal like a strawtail hovering.

Dance, she danced, against the hypocrites and the liars and the pillars of the state, thrusting her hips and her breasts at the night inviting the stars to join her in

Dancing for women to live, arms up to the sky, hands parted and blessed

Dancing for women to love, feet feeling the earth below, legs parted and blessed

For the love of men and women and children

For the love of all creatures all living things and all matter

They danced the whole night long

They conjured up the depths of their being and the sources of their life

And they found the roots of their bondage, forgotten to all but their bodies,

And

They danced,

Getting rid of it.

Everyone else had gone. The children were fast asleep on their straw mats.

It was the magic hour. The moon shift was over. But the sun hadn't risen to start to light the day-sky.

There was Nani, whose party it was, and she lived on her own and knew lots of things. Some people said she knew everything, but of course that wasn't possible. Others said she knew a sight too much.

Sadna spoke to her. She said, 'You said, "Be careful of the hole." You said, "I'm going to plant a breadfruit tree in there tomorrow."'

'Yes?' said Nani, meaning, what of it?

'Can we plant it now? There's the loneliness of the night-sky that asks for planting. The hole's already dug. You've already done that for us.'

'Yes, of course. Good idea. Then it'll be all of ours. Then when I get my first breadfruit, you three can come over with all the kids, and we can have it boiled with butter and salt on it for The Boy Who Won't Speak. Or make chips with turmeric on for Giovanni. Or cook one in hot coals for a dessert, with brown sugar down the hole you make after you pull out the stem, for the twins who'll be just the age that loves that.'

'You see the plastic bag over there, Nani? The one with writing on it. Hanging on that hook at the corner of the house?' Sadna asked.

'Yes?'

'Well, we want to bury it, too.'

211

'What's in it then?'

'It's been a problem all day. It's a foetus. Jumila's. We need to bury it. Can we bury it under the breadfruit tree?'

'Are you all right, Jumila? I noticed you danced the abortion dance, or was it the miscarriage dance? The dance of a lost pregnancy,' said Nani. 'You all right?'

'I'm fine now. Just a bit weak and thirsty.'

'You lie down on the bed and close your eyes. This isn't a problem. Of course, we'll bury it. Under the breadfruit tree. Bring the bag in, Sadna. We must look at it, so we know what we're burying. You just stay lying down, keep your eyes closed gently, if you want to, and we'll tell you what we see, Jumila. Is that all right? Then we'll bury it.'

And so she took the Priba Paradise bag, and took the Air Islands Duty Free bag out of it, and put it on the first bag, and then she took the blue one-rupee plastic bag out of the second bag, and put it on both bags, and then she took the foetus out, by its feet, and put it and the afterbirth on all three bags. On her bed. With care and respect.

She spoke in a droning tone. From another world.

'Its legs and arms would have been fine.'

Unconsciously she had started with the legs. Jumila put her hand to her light foot.

'Fingers and toes would have been, too. A big head. Maybe a clever one. It's a girl foetus. Unusual time to lose it at. Four or five months. Most unusual. If it came down on its own. I'll wrap it in a bit of this nice soft old tablecloth.' She tore a square off, in fast movements of her right hand.

212

Rip rip rip. She asked no questions. Why should she?

'Let's go outside for burying it.'

Which they did.

Goldilox Soo climbed into the four-foot cubed hole. And she put it inside and climbed out.

They each put some earth on top of it.

'Rest in peace,' said Nani.

'As we put our next clod of earth in, let's make a vow,' said Jumila.

Sadna and Goldilox looked puzzled.

'Should we vow to help Jayamani with whatever she needs? She has suffered much more than me. Victim of our past confusion and apathy and carelessness. What you think?'

They did vow.

Nani, who didn't know who they were talking about, listened attentively nevertheless, and said that that sounded like a nice vow. She gave her blessing. In confidence.

Then Jumila said, 'Can I plant the breadfruit tree?' Surprising how she recovered like that. Determined to plant the tree.

'Need about another foot of aerated earth first,' said Nani. And so they rained earth in, and rained earth in, half filling the hole.

Jumila carried the breadfruit tree carefully in its black plastic bag to the hole. Climbed down into the hole, feet on the outskirts of the dug hole for respect.

With scissors she cut the bottom of the bag away slowly, so that the earth wouldn't suddenly leave the roots.

'Where did you get the tree from?' Goldilox Soo asked.

'From Maybur. I went and cut the root from the mother tree, and left it for three months to get its own root-system and be independent. Then I went and dug it up, with its sandy soil, and put it in this plastic bag. Then, after the trip here, I let it rest and settle down for six weeks. And now it's getting a good place tonight. Or should I say this morning?'

By now Jumila had chosen the direction the tree would look. The others all started pushing earth in. She had to stay in the hole until the last minute. Then they pulled her out. And put earth back in, leaving the tree in a nice hollow, so its water would collect around it.

Goldilox Soo had already started carrying water from the drum in two buckets.

'You water it first, Nani. Now you, Jumila.'

The Boy Who Won't Speak had woken up.

'Now you, Tibye,' said Goldilox Soo.

When he watered the breadfruit tree, they distinctly heard him say, 'Sister.' They all looked at him in wonder.

Sadna called Jumila aside. 'I've been thinking. And I've thought. I've made a decision. I'll delay declaring the twins. Count forty days from today. On that day, I'm going to declare them. Think about it. If you want to, you can have one. Either the boy or the girl. You tell me after you've

214

thought about it. Then you can declare one and I can declare the other. If you don't say anything to me by the time forty days has passed, I'll keep both, of course. The boy was fathered by a mountain and the girl by the reef. You can choose. I love them both. Could never choose between them, myself. But two is difficult. So, if you want to, you can.'

'I'll see,' she said.

But anyone could tell that, at the end of forty days, she would accept. Anyone can tell she would accept the one fathered by the reef. Anyway The Boy Who Won't Speak had spoken. Tibye had made a request.

For further information about Granta Books
and a full list of titles, please write to us at

Granta Books

2/3 HANOVER YARD

NOEL ROAD

LONDON

N1 8BE

enclosing a stamped, addressed envelope

———————————

You can visit our website at

http://www.granta.com